"Maybe our duck could race your dad and brother's duck?"

Shay's small son studied Natalie as if he couldn't quite decide what to make of her offer. Then he took her hand and walked with her.

"Oh, good. I'm so glad you're here to help me." Natalie gave Shay a smile that made his insides do crazy things.

"Are you guys ready?"

"Oh, right." Shay forced himself to focus on the duck and not Natalie's playful smile.

"Okay, on my count. One, two, three. Go!" she yelled.

At the last second, Natalie and Liam's duck surged ahead and toppled off the trough and into the bin at the other end.

"Great job, buddy." She scooped Liam up and twirled him around. "We did it."

Liam tipped his face to the sky, giggling as he clutched the sleeves of her sweater.

Shay's heart expanded at the sheer joy on Liam's face and Natalie's willingness to jump in and play.

Didn't she know how much she meant to them already?

How much she meant to him?

Heidi McCahan is a Pacific Northwest girl at heart, but now resides in North Carolina with her husband and three boys. When she isn't writing inspirational romance novels, Heidi can usually be found reading a book, enjoying a cup of coffee and avoiding the laundry pile. She's also a huge fan of dark chocolate and her adorable goldendoodle, Finn. She enjoys connecting with readers, so please visit her website, heidimccahan.com.

Books by Heidi McCahan

Love Inspired

The Firefighter's Twins

The Firefighter's Twins

Heidi McCahan

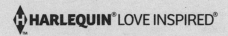

HARLEQUIN® LOVE INSPIRED®

Recycling programs for this product may not exist in your area.

LOVE INSPIRED BOOKS

ISBN-13: 978-1-335-42815-8

The Firefighter's Twins

www.Harlequin.com

Printed in U.S.A.

Trust in the Lord with all thine heart;
and lean not unto thine own understanding.
In all thy ways acknowledge Him,
and He shall direct thy paths.
—*Proverbs* 3:5–6

To Davis, Leland, Jonah, Micah, Eli and Luke,
who inspired the twin boys in this novel.
Thank you. May you continue to spread joy
and laughter wherever you go.

Chapter One

Natalie McDowell paced the courtyard in front of the white clapboard barn, her stomach twisted in knots. As the silver BMW convertible turned down the magnolia-lined drive, she swiped her clammy palms against the skirt of her navy blue sundress. *You've got this. Treat her like any other potential client.* Only that was the problem. This wasn't just any client. Karen Thomas owned Forever Love, North Carolina's premier event planning firm. She'd asked to schedule a consultation and a walk-through. What did she want with Magnolia Lane?

Determined to be prepared for any possible scenario, Natalie had stayed up well past midnight, ensuring every inch of the restored livery was fit for royalty.

Easing to a stop, the woman behind the wheel flashed a bright smile and offered a casual wave.

Natalie waved back, silently praying her legs would stop quaking before Karen stepped out of her car.

"Hello," the petite blonde called as she emerged, tanned and flawless in her white slacks and silky red blouse. She thrust out a French-manicured hand. "Karen Thomas, from Forever Love. You must be Natalie."

"A pleasure to meet you, Karen." Natalie shook her hand. "Welcome to Magnolia Lane."

"Thank you. I appreciate you taking the time to meet with me today. I'm sure you're quite busy with fall weddings." Karen pivoted, scanning her surroundings. "This is stunning."

Natalie struggled to maintain her neutral expression. Karen Thomas just called her little old barn *stunning*. She drew a deep breath and gestured toward the building and adjacent courtyard. "We're very proud of it. Brides and grooms alike find it's the perfect blend of modern yet rustic."

"I agree." Karen strode toward the entrance. "There's nothing else like it nearby, correct?"

The walkie-talkie resting on top of Natalie's iPad nearby squawked to life. "Natalie, we've got a code stork. I repeat, code stork near the corn maze."

No. Adrenaline pulsed through her veins. "Karen, excuse me. I'm so sorry. I've got to go. A woman's about to give birth in the corn maze."

Karen's perfect brow knitted together. "But I—"

"I'm sorry. Truly, I am. Feel free to walk through and see if this might be a good fit. I'll be back in fifteen minutes." She scooped up the iPad and walkie-talkie, and then she jogged toward her golf cart parked beside the barn, her cowboy boots clicking against the cobblestones.

"Nat, where are you? Her water broke." Shelby, the college student supervising the birthday party, had more than enough experience to manage a crisis, but this was uncharted territory. Not even Rex, their most seasoned employee, could deliver a human in a corn maze.

"Call an ambulance." Natalie slid behind the wheel. "I'll be there in two minutes."

"Copy that. Please hurry." Shelby's panicked voice crackled through the speaker.

She set the iPad and the walkie-talkie on the cushioned seat next to her, put the cart in gear and stomped on the pedal. While she careened down the gravel path, her mind raced. Several of the off-duty firefighters from the station down the road were attending a birthday party at the farm today. Surely they were qualified to handle emergency childbirth.

"Oh, dear Lord, please don't let her give birth in front of a bunch of three-year-olds. Make a way for the ambulance to get through the crowd." Her prayers were like that these days—flung up in tense moments, desperate submissions shot heavenward, while her plans unraveled like a loose thread. God heard her, but He hadn't responded like she'd anticipated. Still she longed for a sign, a clear indication it was time to chase her dreams. Would she ever get a chance to focus exclusively on wedding planning, instead of dealing with the relentless flood of issues facing Glenview Farms?

She'd thrown herself into managing the farm and launching Magnolia Lane, desperate for an avenue to both channel her grief and help her forget about Spencer. His sudden death on duty at the fire department two years ago had leveled her. And cured her of any desire to ever date another firefighter. Her work might've saved her, but it also meant Mama and Daddy depended on her to keep things running. Especially now that Daddy's health was declining.

A bead of sweat trickled down Natalie's spine as she steered the cart around a group of guests snapping selfies by the old tobacco barn, their faces flushed from the heat. For the third Saturday in September, summer hadn't shown any interest in giving up and making way for fall.

Near the entrance to the corn maze, a very pregnant woman clutched her lower back and paced in a small circle. Shelby hovered near her elbow, a cell phone to her ear, while a crowd of onlookers gathered around. Natalie stopped the cart and hopped out, side-stepping identical twin boys fighting over a pinwheel. They couldn't have been more than two, judging by the pacifiers wedged securely in their mouths.

"Shelby, I'm here. What can I do?" Natalie joined

them, wincing as the pregnant woman stopped pacing and squeezed her eyes shut.

"I—I don't know." Shelby's voice wobbled, and she cast a furtive glance toward the woman. "This is Maria. She's expecting her second baby any minute now. I'm staying on the line with the dispatcher until the ambulance gets here."

"Perfect. I'll redirect the kids to the inflatables. Maybe if they're bouncing, the siren won't scare them." She whirled around and walked straight into a firm, defined chest clad in a navy University of Virginia T-shirt. Her gaze traveled up to an angular jaw, tan skin and moss green eyes staring down from beneath the brim of a well-loved ball cap. A warm hand on her bare forearm steadied her.

"Ma'am? Is there anything I can do to help?"

His deep voice made her insides dip and swerve. She moistened her dry-as-sandpaper mouth. "Are you a doctor?"

"No. A firefighter. My kids are guests at the birthday party." He cut his gaze toward the expectant mother. "Do you have a place where she can lie down?"

"Lie down? I was hoping the ambulance would—"

"Oh, my—" Maria's voice trailed off, and Natalie sneaked a peek over her shoulder. Maria grimaced, her fingers splayed across her protruding abdomen.

The man let go of Natalie's arm and stepped away, pressing his thumb and index finger to his lips. He released a shrill whistle that stopped all conversation. "Hey, folks. Let me have your attention, please."

The wail of a siren grew louder, but all eyes remained fixed on him.

"Wait," Natalie hissed. "What are you doing?"

"Taking charge."

"But I'm—"

"Trent, line the children up behind your daughter and head over to the inflatables so we can get this ambulance in here. Hamilton, you're in charge of finding Maria's husband and daughter. Start at the restrooms."

"Got it." Cell phone in hand, Hamilton jogged away.

"One, two, three, eyes on me." Trent Walker, Natalie's friend and another local firefighter, held his hand high in the air. "Anyone who wants to go to the bounce house, line up behind Ella."

The children maneuvered into a disjointed line behind Trent's daughter. She wore a princess dress and tiara, clearly enjoying her role as the birthday girl. Even the boys tussling over the pinwheel obeyed, bringing up the rear as adults and children moved across the grass toward the inflatables.

"Wow." Shelby's eyes widened. "Impressive."

Natalie was speechless.

Shay turned his attention back to Maria. "I'm Shay Campbell. I work for the fire department. Do you know if you're having a boy or a girl?"

"Another girl." Maria gasped, swiping her forearm across her glistening brow.

"Wonderful. When's your due date?"

"Yesterday." Pain rippled across her features. "My first one didn't come this fast."

"Hang on. We're going to help you." Shay looked from Maria to Natalie. "Bring the golf cart closer. We've got to move her."

"Move her where?"

He pointed toward the parking lot. "We'll meet the ambulance at the gate."

She turned around, looking past the rows and rows of cars in the field to the access gate at the far end of their property. A figure wearing Glenview's signature yellow T-shirt maneuvered the heavy metal bar out of the way, and an ambulance eased through, siren howling as the red lights flashed. Glenview's staff was following emergency protocol—just like they'd rehearsed half a dozen times.

"Ma'am?" Shay prompted. "I think we'd better act quickly."

She pivoted back toward him. "Are you sure moving her is the best idea? We've trained our staff to guide the ambulance right—"

Ignoring her question, he brushed past her, guiding Maria toward the golf cart. Sweat dampened the back of his snug-fitting T-shirt as he helped her onto the second seat. Natalie's eyes swept from the expanse of his shoulders to his gray cargo shorts and muscular legs. Most of the firefighters attending the birthday party with their families had come by the farm to eat lunch at The Grille several times, but she'd never seen Shay before.

He whirled around and caught her staring. "C'mon, we don't have time to argue."

Heat singed her cheeks. "I'm not arguing. I'm trying to tell you we can get the ambulance over here. We've done it before. What about her husband and daughter? You want me to leave without them?"

He silenced her with his fierce gaze. "Just drive, please. Hamilton will figure it out."

She slid behind the wheel again, her heart pounding. Shay stayed with Maria, coaching her in a calm yet firm voice as Natalie sped across the grass toward the ambulance.

"Breathe, Maria. I know the contractions are coming hard and fast, but you've got to try to breathe."

Maria grunted out a response and then panted.

Natalie cringed when they hit a rut, bouncing over it. "I'm sorry. So sorry."

"Oh, my—" Maria's words were lost as she released a guttural moan. "I think I need to push. I really, really need to push."

"No," Natalie and Shay said in unison.

"We're almost there. You do not want to have this baby in a golf cart, right? Everything you need is inside that ambulance." Shay's confident voice never wavered, but Natalie's mind spun out of control with possibilities, making her mash down harder on the accelerator. They'd assisted guests with heat exhaustion, chest pain, sprained ankles… even the occasional broken arm. But a baby delivered in her golf cart? That was ten times worse than the corn maze. She gritted her teeth. *Moving Maria was a horrible idea. Why did I listen to him?*

They reached the ambulance, and two EMTs jumped out, each securing blue disposable gloves on their hands.

"C'mon, Maria. Let's get you to the hospital." Shay helped her from the cart and handed her off to the closest guy in uniform. Natalie got out and hovered behind them, catching pieces of their conversation. Something about the timing of the contractions and when her water broke—all the details she should've noted, had she not been so exasperated by this mysterious firefighter who happened upon the scene and took control.

Despite her resistance to lying down or leaving without her family, they had Maria secured on the stretcher and inside the ambulance in a matter of seconds. Once her husband and daughter caught up and were on board, the EMTs slammed the doors and whisked her away, lights flashing but no sirens. Would they even make it off the property before the baby arrived?

Shay watched them go and then turned to face her. His gaze narrowed. "Y'all need to reevaluate your emergency action plan. That could've been a disaster."

A terse response flitted through her brain. She tipped her chin up. "It could've been, but it wasn't. I guess the good Lord was looking out for us. And Maria, too."

A muscle in his jaw knotted tight. "How many pregnant women visit your farm? You need to be prepared for more scenarios like this one."

She fixed him with a pointed stare. "We are more than prepared to handle a crisis. If you would've listened and let me execute our emergency action plan, we could've skipped the golf cart altogether." Without waiting for his answer, she climbed back in the golf cart and drove away.

"'Y'all need a better emergency action plan.'" She mimicked his deep Southern drawl as she drove back toward the barn to smooth things over with Karen, if she was even still there. Who did Shay think he was, anyway, jumping in and taking over? So what if he'd helped avert a crisis. Did he have to be so smug about it? She made a mental note to email Chief Murphy later and ask who he'd assigned to serve on the fall festival committee and help with their service project. If it was Shay Campbell, she'd request Trent instead.

This fall marked her family's tenth season of offering a destination farm experience, complete with hay rides, the corn maze and several other creative opportunities to get kids outside. They took every reasonable precaution to protect their guests. She blew out a long breath. The last thing she needed was some arrogant firefighter telling her how to run her own farm…or her fall festival committee.

Shay watched her drive off, her honey-brown hair spilling between the skinny straps of her sundress. Despite the medical emergency, the curve of her bronzed, bare shoulders and delicate collarbone hadn't escaped his notice. He'd always had a thing for sundresses and cowboy boots. Until Monica left. He'd stopped listening to the country radio station for fear he'd hear her latest hit single.

Shoving aside the memory of his ex-wife, he jogged back toward the inflatables. Isn't that where he instructed the other parents to take the kids? But when he got to the giant multicolored bounce house, the kids seemed older. Bigger. He scanned the faces of the adults hovering on the grassy area nearby. This was only his second week in Meadow Springs, but none of these ladies looked like anybody he'd met at the beginning of the party. Not that he had much time for small talk. He'd left the socializing up to his mother, while he kept a vigilant watch on the boys. If he looked away for an instant, Liam and Aiden toddled off, climbing something, touching things they shouldn't—making his heart race. He'd lost focus once before, and it had cost his family dearly. He couldn't afford not to be hypervigilant.

He spun in a circle, searching for towheaded boys wearing denim shorts and blue and green T-shirts. *Don't panic. Mom can handle it.* But this was their first birthday party that wasn't limited to close family members. Would she remember to ask about the ingredients and double-check the labels? And could she deal with the tantrums if she had to tell the boys they couldn't have any?

"Excuse me." He spoke to an older woman who appeared to be supervising the inflatables. "Do you know where the little kids from the birthday party went? A bunch of two-and three-year-olds?"

She fluffed her short brown hair with her fingers and smiled, staring at him over the rim of her leopard-print sunglasses. "Shelby's group?"

"Yes, ma'am."

"They've gone on to the gazebo. They were afraid of the siren, so Shelby skipped straight to cake and ice cream."

"Where's the gazebo?"

She pointed behind him. "Go toward the pond and past the rubber duck races. You can't miss it, hon."

"Thank you." He weaved around couples with strollers, kids tugging on their parents' hands and packs of teenagers staring at their phones. Gravel crunched under his tennis shoes as he made his way past the main building. The aroma of fries and hamburgers filled the air, making his stomach rumble. He'd worry about lunch later. His boys' safety was his first priority.

A line snaked out the door of the café. "Pardon me, please." He eased between two women chatting in line, while two little girls chased each other in circles around their legs. Once he was past the crowd, a large white gazebo situated next to a pond came into view. A group of older boys cranked the handles on the water pumps nearby, their rubber ducks racing down the water-filled troughs. Aiden and Liam would love that. Maybe if they had time, he'd bring them over to check it out.

Moms and dads mingled with the children in the gazebo, talking and laughing. A few glanced up as he joined the party. Walker and Harrison stood by a cooler with cans of soda in their hands. He'd thank them for their help with Maria in a minute, once he knew Mom had handled the cake situation.

"Shay," Mom called out from where she sat at the end of a long picnic table, Aiden and Liam across from her.

"Da-da!" Aiden shrieked, his blue eyes gleaming. Frosting coated his fingers and ringed his mouth. The paper plate in front of him held a half-eaten slice of cake and a melting scoop of vanilla ice cream. Liam didn't even look up, all his attention centered on loading his fork with the sugary treats.

Shay's stomach lurched. "Mom. The cake—" He raced to the table, reaching for the boys' plates.

"Sweetie, I scoured the labels and interrogated the poor girls serving it. It's fine. No peanuts."

Aiden's lower lip quivered, and he snatched the plate back, glaring. "Mine."

"We don't know if it's safe for you to eat, buddy. Let me check."

Mom sighed. "I promise I double—"

Her words were drowned out by the sound of the boys crying. Not a little crying, either. The kind of sobbing that stopped all conversation.

"Hey, fellas." A young woman approached the table carrying an ice-cream carton and scoop. "Is everything okay?"

"Aiden has a severe peanut allergy, and I don't let Liam eat peanuts, just to be safe." Shay felt the curious stares of the other guests as the boys continued wailing. "I was concerned about cross-contamination."

"My daughter's the birthday girl. She has a severe allergy, too. Trust me, I can guarantee this cake is completely acceptable." She set the ice-cream container on the table. "I'm Caroline Walker, by the way. You probably know my husband, Trent, from the station."

Man, he felt like an idiot. He wished the ground would open and swallow him whole. Shay dropped his gaze to the boys' plates. "Here you go, boys. I'm sorry. Daddy messed up." He slid the plates back in front of them. "Go ahead. You can eat it." He offered his hand to Caroline. "Thanks for clarify-

ing. I'm Shay Campbell, and this is Aiden, Lia
and my mother, Belinda Campbell."

"Nice to meet you." Caroline shook his hand.
"Do you mind if they have more ice cream? We
bought way too much."

Aiden and Liam's pathetic sniffles disappeared
as they shot cautious glances in Shay's direction.
"It's fine. You may have more."

The conversation around him ebbed and flowed
again, much to his relief.

"See?" Mom patted their little hands. "Everything's going to be okay. By the time you're finished with that yummy cake and ice cream, I bet it
will be time to watch Ella open presents."

"We're glad y'all could come today." Caroline
added a tiny scoop of ice cream to Aiden's plate,
and he grinned up at her.

"Thanks for the invitation. This is quite a treat."
He'd been counting the minutes until the party
ended and he could get the boys home for nap time.
More ice cream would probably derail their afternoon routine. But a sugar high was a small price
to pay for inflicting such pain on his innocent little
boys. They'd suffered enough already.

"Are you all getting settled in your new place?
Trent said you're in that neighborhood behind the
farm?"

Shay nodded. "Meadow Crossing. Yeah, it's…
great." He pictured the moving boxes still stacked
against the wall in the detached garage. Sometime

soon he'd carve out time to tackle those. Getting the boys settled in their new bedroom and unpacking their toys was as far as he'd gotten. Well, that and the kitchen essentials. Even with Mom's help, establishing a new routine and helping them cope with Monica's absence was all he could do.

"How about you, Mrs. Campbell? Are you close by?"

"My husband and I live in the new retirement community a little closer to town. But I stay with the boys when Shay's at the station."

He grimaced. Did she have to tell everybody about that? It wasn't a secret that he didn't have a wife, but the looks of sympathy and awkward silence that usually followed made him uncomfortable.

If Caroline was surprised by the revelation, she hid it well. "That's wonderful. We have family nearby, too. It's such a blessing, especially when the guys are on duty. This is a great group of people, Shay. We treat each other like family, so if you need anything, let us know."

"Thanks. I will." He forced a smile, ignoring Mom's triumphant look.

"I better serve some more ice cream. Oh, wait." Caroline surveyed the gazebo. "Huh. That's weird. I thought for sure she'd stop by. I wanted to introduce you to Natalie McDowell."

Shay's gut clenched. He wasn't here to make new friends. "That's okay. I'm not exactly—"

"I heard Chief Murphy assigned you to her fall festival committee. I thought you might want to say hello before the first meeting." Caroline shrugged. "She manages this farm. I'm sure things are hectic today, with Maria almost giving birth and all. Maybe she'll stop by later."

Visions of a sundress, boots and a golf cart raced through his mind. *Uh-oh.* Based on their previous interaction, she'd be less than thrilled about his assigned role. He wasn't really crazy about it, either. Working closely with an attractive young woman only put him and his broken heart on a pointless trajectory. Between Monica's sudden departure, the move from Virginia and caring for two toddlers, there wasn't space in his life for a new relationship. He couldn't fathom falling in love again, anyway. Especially not with someone as strong-willed and determined as Natalie.

Chapter Two

After attending the early service at church the next morning, Natalie sat at her kitchen table, eating a sandwich while scrolling through her email on her iPad. There were a hundred things to do today, and all she really wanted was a quiet afternoon at home. And possibly a nap.

A message from Forever Love dropped into her inbox. She stopped chewing and let her finger hover over the screen. Did she even want to read this right now? Her brief meeting with Karen after the Maria debacle had ended on a cryptic note. While Karen had taken several pictures with her phone and asked plenty of questions, she'd driven away after offering a quick handshake and the standard "we'll be in touch."

Oh, why not. What did she have to lose? She opened the message.

"'Dear Natalie,'" she read out loud, "'it was wonderful to meet with you and see your delightful venue. Magnolia Lane is everything I hoped it would be.'"

Natalie's pulse sped as she devoured the rest of the message silently. "Forever Love is actively working to expand its reach into the greater Raleigh area. Our research indicates this market has tremendous potential. We have a proposition we believe you'll find very appealing. Our firm is interested in acquiring your business. Secondly, we'd like to offer you a position as an event planner here in our Charlotte office..."

Natalie gasped. "What in the world?" She read the details again. *Sell Magnolia Lane?* The thought had never crossed her mind. But working for an elite firm like Forever Love—now *that* she'd dreamed about often, especially in the lean times when she'd struggled to open Magnolia Lane. Having someone else in her corner to brainstorm strategies for dealing with high-maintenance brides, or share the burden of upkeep and help secure new vendors when the caterer went out of business... Forever Love's proposition felt like a breath of fresh air.

Easy. Natalie heeded the warning in her head and forced herself to focus on the message's closing lines. "My business partner and I would like to give you some time to consider our offer. If you're available, we'd like to discuss this via a video conference call on Thursday, October 2, at 1:00 p.m.

Please respond at your convenience and indicate your availability…"

"Yes, yes, I'm available." Natalie's fingers trembled as she clicked over to her digital calendar and scrolled to October 2. Even though it was less than two weeks away, thankfully she was still free. She scheduled the call with Forever Love.

A dozen questions flew through her mind, but a quick glance at the clock revealed she had all of five minutes to get out the door and over to The Grille to make sure Nolan, the new manager, was prepared for the after-church lunch rush. If he had everything under control, she'd have just enough time to walk across the highway to the fall festival committee meeting.

After typing a brief response and accepting the meeting request, Natalie pushed back her chair and tucked her iPad inside her handbag. Striding to the sink, she added her plate to the dirty dishes already stacked on the counter. Chores would have to wait. She cast a longing glance toward her bungalow's cozy living room as she headed for the front door. Sunlight streamed through the wide front window, spilling onto the overstuffed cushions of her favorite chair and a stack of untouched novels she'd intended to read before the hectic fall season started. Those would have to wait, too.

With a heavy sigh, she shifted her focus to the mirror in the entryway, frowning at her reflection. A string of late nights and early mornings hadn't done her complexion any favors. She fished a tube of lip gloss out from the depths of her bag, and then she dabbed on a quick coat and surveyed the results. Good enough. Natalie readjusted the coral scarf layered over her white T-shirt and navy cardigan and then slipped out the front door.

Outside, her porch swing swayed in the breeze. She drew in a deep breath—crisp, cool air and no humidity. Birds chirped, while the familiar rumble of a tractor echoed across the otherwise empty fields. She shouldered her bag again as she walked down the steps and across the yard.

"Hey, there, sunshine," her sister Kirsten called out from the parking lot, wearing a stylish, belted denim dress and short, open-toed suede boots. She clasped Daddy's elbow with one hand, while Mama assisted him on his left side. "We thought we'd have lunch here today."

"Great." Natalie pasted on a smile, determined to mask her heartache. Daddy hadn't made eye contact yet, his focus on the gravel in front of him as he struggled to walk the short distance from the car to the front door.

"Hey, Mama and Daddy." Natalie held the door open for them. "I bet Nolan has your favorite table ready."

Daddy met her gaze briefly, a twinkle evident in his blue eyes. "Sure hope so."

Mama squeezed Natalie's arm as they passed. "Hey, sugar."

Natalie followed them inside. The aroma of fried food lingered in the air, even though the restaurant didn't open until twelve thirty on Sundays. The dining area sat empty, although it wouldn't stay that way for long. While Mama and Daddy made their way to a corner booth near the windows with a beautiful view of the pond, Natalie tugged on Kirsten's short sleeve.

"What's the occasion?"

Kirsten lingered near the door. "What do you mean?"

"Mama and Daddy haven't been here for lunch in weeks."

Kirsten sighed. "I wanted Mama to have a break from fixing a meal. They used to love to go out for lunch after church, but Daddy says he gets too worn out. I convinced them to come here, since they're only two minutes from the house."

Natalie watched Mama help him maneuver into the booth. "We're going to have to talk to them about assisted living. Soon."

"Go for it. I've tried bringing it up. Mama shuts me down every time."

Natalie turned away, her stomach clenched in a tight knot. Daddy's mobility had declined more rapidly than she'd expected. "I don't understand how they can ignore the facts. He's getting worse. We can't pretend his health isn't going to impact their lifestyle."

"I know. But Mama thinks she can handle it.

Like she handles everything—by sheer force and stubborn determination."

"What if she's not able?" Natalie threaded her scarf between her fingers. "Eventually he'll need care, possibly around-the-clock. Sure, the farm's doing well, but the liability insurance and property taxes get more expensive every year. What if the cost of his care exceeds their income?"

Kirsten's eyes glistened with tears. "Believe me, I've thought about everything you've mentioned. Mama and Daddy simply don't want to hear it."

"If Daddy's diagnosis isn't…" Natalie swallowed hard. She couldn't bring herself to say the words. "If the news isn't what we'd hoped, I think we should be prepared to have that hard conversation. Cami's in school at Clemson, you're working on your MBA and I'm practically working two jobs. Tisha's not here, right—"

"Mama says Tisha's coming back from Alaska in the next week or so," Kirsten said.

Natalie sighed. "Tisha's been away a long time. She can't exactly make an educated choice about what's best." She stopped short of mentioning how their sister's ridiculous plan to lease some of their land to that solar energy company nearly cost them everything.

"She's changed a lot since she moved away, Nat." Kirsten shifted from one foot to the other. "Mama and Daddy are her parents, too. We can't exclude her from the discussion."

Natalie clamped her mouth closed. She couldn't argue with that. Although Tisha's blind affection for her conniving ex-boyfriend and careless actions almost ruined any future plans for the farm, Natalie couldn't be too critical. Not with the surprise news from Forever Love sitting in her inbox. If she decided to accept their offer, she'd be moving to Charlotte. What if the sale of Magnolia Lane helped provide professional caregivers? Then they wouldn't have to worry about financing Daddy's care. On the other hand, it meant pursuing her dreams at the expense of her family's heritage. Daddy's parents had built the barn themselves. Even if they'd deeded the building and the surrounding land to her, the news of the sale would still come as a shock. Could she really live with that?

Kirsten's gaze flitted from Natalie to Mama and Daddy. "Let's wait and see what the doctor says before we try to talk to them again. Maybe it's not as bad as we think."

"Miss Natalie?"

Natalie glanced over Kirsten's shoulder to see Nolan, who was hurrying toward her as he tied an apron over faded jeans and an NC State T-shirt.

"I was fixin' to text you. Justine called in sick. Any chance you could fill in at the register during the lunch rush?"

Oh, brother. What other surprises could land in

her path today? "I'll find somebody to help out, Nolan. Thanks for letting me know."

"Yes, ma'am." He returned to the kitchen.

Kirsten frowned. "Are you short-handed all day? I'd offer to help, but—"

"Could you? I've got my first fall festival committee in a few minutes." She regretted the request as soon as she said it. Maybe having Kirsten fill in for Justine wasn't the best idea. Her sisters hadn't worked the counter in ages. Natalie bit her lip. What if she pushed back the meeting until—

"I guess I can do it. I'll work on my presentation later…"

Natalie shoved her doubts aside. It would have to do for now. "Perfect. Thank you so much." Natalie didn't stick around. If she lingered, she'd be tempted to tell Kirsten everything about Forever Love, and it was too soon for that. She needed more information. More time to weigh her options. She rubbed at the ache in her chest as she hurried toward the door. A solution that appealed to everyone and allowed her to follow her dream felt hopelessly out of reach.

Outside, she offered friendly greetings to the customers coming into The Grille, recognizing several familiar faces. Mama and Daddy would be glad to see some of their friends. A line of at least a dozen cars waited on the two-lane road beside the entrance to the farm, blinkers on, indicating they'd be pulling into the parking lot. Looked like another busy Sunday afternoon. That would make Mama and Daddy happy, too.

Her smile quickly faded once she jogged across the road to the new subdivision where the committee meeting was scheduled to take place.

Shay Campbell was less than twenty feet away, climbing out of a pickup truck.

Natalie's steps faltered, and she stumbled, wincing more from embarrassment than from the twinge in her ankle. What was he doing here?

Shay waved, a smile lifting one corner of his mouth.

Natalie tried to play it cool while her pulse went all kinds of crazy. Although she hated to admit it, he did look handsome in khaki slacks and a brick red button-down, the sleeves rolled up to reveal his chiseled forearms.

"Hey." Shay closed the driver's door. "Is this the fall festival committee meeting?"

She cocked her to head to one side. "It's supposed to be. The others aren't here yet."

"Mind if I join you? I'm not on duty today, but the chief sent me as the liaison from the fire department."

Rats. Why him? The chief had ignored her email requesting Trent Walker's help.

He shoved his hands in his pockets. "He said we needed to have a presence at major community events."

"You must've drawn the short straw."

"I don't understand."

"Two of our key members and biggest supporters of the festival had to step down unexpectedly. They're in Chicago caring for their daughter and her family. We're going to struggle to pull the festival together without them."

A frown etched his features. "Unless Chief Murphy tells me differently, the fire department is committed to helping. When's the festival?"

"In about six weeks. The first Saturday in November."

"One of the guys mentioned a service project. Is this it?" He angled his head toward the lot nearby.

"Yes." Natalie glanced at the concrete foundation and exposed wood framework for the walls. Mounds of ugly red clay and large rocks dug up by the construction crew surrounded what would eventually be a three-bedroom rambler. Nothing much had changed since the last time she'd stopped by. Had the volunteers run into a problem no one had mentioned to her?

"Is anyone managing the project?"

"That's where things get complicated. I guess I'm in charge now." She sighed and met his gaze again. For the second time in one weekend, the luminous color of his eyes—green rimmed with hints of blue—captured her attention.

A girl could get lost in those eyes.

Shay's brow arched, waiting for her to elaborate. Warmth heated her skin. "The house is for a wounded veteran and his family. The big reveal happens during the festival. At least, that was the plan, anyway. Now with Maureen, the former committee chairperson, gone—"

The sound of another car approaching interrupted her. Natalie glanced over her shoulder to see her best friend, Erin, parking beside the curb.

"Wait." Shay held up his hand. "Before the others get here, I have something I need to say."

"Oh?" Natalie faced him again and tucked a strand of hair behind her ear. *This should be interesting.* "I'm listening."

"I—I owe you an apology."

"For?"

"I'm sorry for the way I spoke to you at the farm. I shouldn't have been so critical."

"Apology accepted." She reached into her bag for her iPad. "Have you heard how Maria's doing?"

"I have." He offered a sheepish smile. "She had a healthy baby girl in the ambulance, on the way to the hospital."

"Whoa. That was quick."

"Very quick. If it weren't for that stellar emergency plan of yours, she might've delivered in the middle of the party."

"So you recognize my plan wasn't so flawed, after all?" She couldn't resist a subtle jab. Or conceal her smile.

"I do. I mean, I recognize that your plan isn't so

flawed. At all. Again, I apologize for being rude and trying to take control of the situation."

She lifted one shoulder. It was kind of fun to see him stumble over his words. "Don't worry about it. But thank you for apologizing."

"You're welcome." He studied the lot again. "Any idea what you still need in terms of building supplies? You've got walls up, it's framed…looks like the subflooring was started. What would it take to finish this in time for the festival?"

About fifty more volunteers and an extra three weeks. She bit back her snide reply as Erin strode toward them, a pastry box and a stack of napkins in hand.

"Hey." Erin's curious gaze flitted from Natalie to Shay and back. "What's going on?"

Natalie pretended not to notice Erin's nonverbal cues. No doubt they'd exchange a flurry of text messages later about the newest member of their committee. "Shay, have you met Erin Taylor? She and her husband own the coffee shop in town."

He shook Erin's outstretched hand. "Shay Campbell. It's nice to meet you."

"Nice to meet you, too." Erin let go of his hand and then pressed her palm over the napkins on top of the white cardboard box to keep them from blowing away. "Are you building in this neighborhood?"

"Not exactly. I'm a volunteer committee member from the fire department. Natalie was bringing me up to speed on the status of the service project." Shay's arm brushed against hers, and the scent of something clean nudged her nose, like laundry soap and fresh air. Natalie's stomach tightened. Why did he have to smell so good?

"Was she?" Erin asked, an innocent smile tugging at her lips. "She's served on the fall festival committee for years. If anyone can whip us into shape and get the job done, it's Natalie."

It was Natalie's turn to fire a pointed gaze Erin's direction. "That's sweet of you to say, but Maureen had much stronger contacts for building supplies and coordinating volunteers. I'm all about weddings and hay rides. Lumber and windows? Not so much."

"Oh, please." Erin playfully nudged Natalie's hip with her own. "You're the logical choice to replace her, especially on short notice. She's only in Chicago while her daughter's recovering from her car accident. It's not like you can't reach her. If I know Maureen, she'll find a way to get you all the information you need. This festival was her pride and joy."

"I just wish we could do more." Natalie frowned. "We could've built three new houses for wounded veterans and their families if we had more resources."

"You only lost Maureen and her husband. There are plenty of other people in Meadow Springs who will gladly help," Erin reminded her.

"I'm grateful for the little bit of progress we've made. I'm just afraid we won't finish in time." Natalie's declaration was punctuated by more car doors slamming. Missy Josephson hurried over, with Pastor Adams not far behind. *Thank You, Lord.* Natalie straightened, the tense knots in her shoulders loosening. She was beginning to think they'd forgotten. "Hey. I'm so glad you're both here."

Missy's purse slid down her arm as she leaned in and gave Natalie a quick hug. "I wouldn't miss it. I'm sorry I'm late. It took forever to get the kids out the door and over to my parents' house." She looked at Shay speaking with Pastor Adams and shot Natalie a questioning glance.

"Missy, Pastor Adams, this is Shay Campbell. Shay, this is Missy Josephson and Rick Adams, the youth pastor from Meadow Springs Community Church."

Once introductions were finished, and they'd all gathered in a half-circle, Natalie perused her notes quickly. "Thank you for coming. I'm sure you've heard two of our committee members have resigned as a result of recent events in their daughter's life. But we've gained a new member, thanks to Chief Murphy at the fire station. I was updating Shay on the building project before you both got here."

Pastor Adams smiled. "We're glad to have you, Shay. The fire department's presence at the festival is always a big favorite."

"Oh, the kids love it." Missy bobbed her head. "My students are already asking if they can squirt the hose and wear those plastic fire hats."

"Missy's a preschool teacher," Natalie said.

Shay smiled. "Little boys love fire engines."

"That sounds like the voice of experience." Erin opened the box to reveal an assortment of her legendary cookies. "Do you have kids, Shay?"

Natalie stilled, pretending to stare at her screen. But her racing pulse was a dead giveaway. She was more curious than she cared to admit. Hadn't he mentioned something about his kids at the birthday party?

"Twin two-year-old boys," Shay said.

Oh, my. Natalie's gaze darted to his ring finger. Nothing. Warmth heated her cheeks. She only needed his help with the festival, right? Shay's family life—particularly his potential single-dad status—was none of her business. The heartache over losing Spencer was enough to last a lifetime. She gave herself a mental shake. *Avoiding firefighters, remember?*

"How about the other trucks we've had in the past?" Pastor Adams chose a chocolate chip cookie from the box. "Kids enjoy climbing all over that stuff."

Bless him for steering the meeting back on track. "We always have a tractor, riding mower and Dad's old pickup truck available." Natalie glanced down and double-checked her notes. "I've left a message with a heavy equipment company in Raleigh to see if they'd bring a loader or a dump truck out. They haven't returned my call."

"Do you want my husband to follow up on that?" Missy whipped out her phone. "He has quite a few contacts through the department of transportation."

"That would be fabulous. Thank you."

"Of course. Let me send him a quick text." Missy's fingers flew over her screen.

Shay declined the cookie Erin offered. "Is there any sort of performance or live entertainment?"

"Yes, that's the best part." Natalie grinned. "Jayce Philips, the hottest new thing in country music, grew up here, and he promised to be our headlining act. Isn't that great?"

Missy gasped. "No way."

"He's a great kid." Pastor Adams nodded his approval.

"I still can't believe it," Natalie said. "His mom indicated he might give away two tickets and backstage passes to his Raleigh concert, too. Wouldn't that be amazing?"

Shay's countenance dimmed.

Natalie studied him. What was wrong? Maybe he didn't like country music. Or he'd never heard of Jayce Philips. If that was even possible.

"Could we auction those tickets off or hold a raffle?" Missy's smile widened, and she snapped her fingers. "Oh, how about this. All proceeds benefit the family moving into the new house."

"Perfect. I'll follow up with Jayce's mom." Natalie typed in a quick note on her to-do list. "Our biggest issue is finishing the house. We've had great support from local volunteer groups, including several men from the church, but it looks like we need even more people to step up. I'm a little concerned that we're running out of time. These next six weeks are crucial."

"I can't officially commit until I talk to some of the guys at the station, but this sounds like the kind of thing we could get involved in," Shay said. "When we aren't on shift, we'd help with the landscaping or the plumbing, hanging drywall—anything we're skilled at doing."

Natalie felt her mouth drop open. "You'd do that? For us?"

"Of course. Like I said, I'd need to ask around. I'm a little new to be volunteering the whole station, but the chief's made it very clear that you will have our full support."

"I—I don't know what to say."

He grinned, warmth returning to his eyes. "Say 'thank you.' Maybe a few cheeseburgers from The Grille would help, too."

"Done." Natalie held his gaze, noting the way a crescent-shaped scar on his cheek accompanied that incredible smile of his.

"I'll schedule some youth group work parties, as well." Pastor Adams dusted crumbs from his fingers. "Our congregation always pulls together when there's a need."

"See? We've got you covered," Missy said. "It's all going to work out."

"I hope you're right." Natalie typed more detailed notes into the app. She still couldn't envision this all coming together in the next month. But she'd never forgive herself if the festival and the service project fell through on her watch. Now that Forever Love's incredible offer had arrived, wooing her with a fantastic opportunity, she'd have to work extra hard to guard against distraction. There was too much on her plate already.

Shay linked his arms across that muscular chest she couldn't seem to get out of her line of sight.

It was time to add "stop staring at handsome service project volunteer" to the top of the to-do list.

Shay corralled Aiden in the bathroom and swept him up in his favorite bath towel—the one with a puppy face and floppy ears on the hood and his name embroidered on the front. "What does a puppy say, Aiden?"

"Woof, woof." Aiden grinned, beads of water from the bath still clinging to his pale eyelashes. That adorable, innocent smile offered a ray of hope—a tender reminder that even in Shay's exhausted state, he could keep going. In moments like these, weary from the marathon of the evening routine, he found himself wishing for a partner—someone to laugh at the boys' antics with, as well as share the load. Natalie's head cocked to one side, her gaze holding his, flitted through his mind.

No.

He gritted his teeth. Who was he kidding? He pushed the mental image aside and shifted his focus back to the boys—where it belonged.

"That's right." He quickly dried Aiden and settled him on the bath mat. "Let's put your jammies on."

"Books?"

"After we brush your teeth, okay?"

"'Kay."

He'd already lifted Liam from the tub, dressed him and sent him across the hall to play in the bedroom. Once he had Aiden's diaper in place, Shay leaned back on his heels and listened.

Silence answered back.

"Liam?" he called over his shoulder. "What are you doing?"

"He play." Aiden stared up at him, fingering the hem of the bath towel lying nearby.

"It doesn't sound like he's playing." He scooped Aiden up, grabbing the clean pajamas off the counter on his way to the door. "Let's go check."

"Yee-um?" Aiden called in a soft voice as they crossed the hallway to the boys' bedroom.

A line of cars and trucks sat abandoned in the middle of the floor, and puzzle pieces were spilled underneath one of the cribs, but there was no sign of Liam.

"Nope, not here." Shifting Aiden to his other hip, Shay hurried down the hall of their modest rambler and stopped at the back door. The dead bolt was secure, so he moved on, checking both the washer and dryer in the laundry room. *Don't panic. He's got to be here somewhere.*

"Where go?" Aiden opened his palm heavenward.

"I don't know. We'll find him." He jogged to the front door and double-checked the childproof knob and the lock. A two-year-old couldn't get past that, right?

He pivoted, raking his hand through his hair as he surveyed the den and breakfast nook. "Liam?" His voice echoed off the empty walls. "Come out, buddy. No more hiding. It's time to read books."

Aiden giggled. "Yee-um hide."

"I'm glad you think it's funny," Shay muttered. His heart rate rising, he retraced his steps back down the hall toward the master bedroom. Once or twice since they'd moved in, he'd allowed the boys to snuggle in bed with him and watch a cartoon on TV. It was the only way he could keep them still while he caught a few more precious minutes of sleep.

"Liam?" He yanked back the comforter on his king-size bed. Empty. His chest tightened. "Where is he, Aiden?"

Aiden regarded him with a wide-eyed stare, his thumb tucked securely in his mouth. This was probably just the beginning of the boys taking up for each other. Shay glanced at the clock on his nightstand. Mom would be over in a few minutes. She could keep Aiden occupied while he searched more thoroughly. Maybe he should call her and ask if she was on her way.

"Sweepy." Aiden mumbled around his thumb, resting his head on Shay's shoulder.

"I know you are. It's almost bedtime. As soon as we find your brother." He patted Aiden's back while he went to the kitchen to grab his phone. When he reached the tile floor, something hard crunched under his bare foot. He stepped back and glanced down. The remnant of a Cheerio was smashed against the tile. A few more dotted the space between him and the pantry door, which was open a fraction of an inch. Shay nudged it open the rest of the way. Liam sat on the pantry floor, surrounded by the cereal—likely the entire box.

"Liam Douglas Campbell, what do you think you're doing?"

"Uh-oh," Aiden whispered.

"Da-da." Liam offered up a Cheerio. "Want some?"

"No, I do not. Get up. Right now." Shay couldn't keep the exasperation from his voice.

Liam clambered to his feet, Cheerios sticking to his dump truck pajamas.

"Daddy mad." Aiden patted Shay's back.

"Daddy is mad. You know better, Liam. You don't go in the pantry without a grown-up, and you certainly don't open anything without asking."

Liam's lower lip pooched out, and he hung his head.

Oh, here we go.

His little body trembled as he began to cry. Out of sympathy, Aiden sniffled a few times before launching the waterworks, squirming to get down. Shay was happy to comply, releasing Aiden to stand with Liam, perhaps in a declaration of solidarity. They stood together, sobbing in the middle of the kitchen floor.

"How did we get here?" he whispered, massaging his aching forehead with his fingertips.

The doorbell rang, which only meant one thing. Backup.

"Let's go see who's here. I sure hope it's Nana." They made their way to the front door, the boys' cries escalating. He was certain that was for Nana's benefit.

He checked the peephole. Mom stood on the porch, holding a grocery sack and her overnight bag. He turned the lock and then opened the door. "Hey, Nana. We're glad you're here."

"Oh, my." Her eyes widened. "What's the matter with my fellas?"

He stepped aside so she could come in. "Someone did some unsupervised exploring in the pantry."

She slid the groceries onto the table, next to a plate with Liam's half-finished supper on it, and set her bag next to the chair. She kneeled down and tugged Liam toward her, smoothing his hair with her hand. He melted against her shoulder, sniffling.

Aiden's tears had slowed, replaced by hiccupy breaths. "Nana. Hugs."

"Pajamas first, pal." Shay glanced around. "Where are they?"

Aiden ignored him, toddling over to nuzzle Nana's other shoulder.

Leaving Mom to soothe the last of their tears, Shay backtracked until he found Aiden's fire truck pajamas on the floor, in the laundry room.

"Here we go, buddy. Let's put these on." Aiden didn't put up any resistance. Shay helped him pull on the shirt and pants, while Mom took Liam over to the couch.

"Why don't we read a few books before bed?" She pulled some of their favorites from the stack on the coffee table.

Shay considered protesting that Liam's misbehavior shouldn't be rewarded. Books were a privilege. But they looked so adorable, snuggled on either side of her, and he was too tired to fight them.

"I'll fix their milk." He trudged to the kitchen, side-stepping the mess on the floor.

Once their sippy cups were full, he returned to the den. Mom was halfway through *The Little Blue*

Truck. Aiden's eyelids drooped, and Liam had already fallen asleep.

She touched a finger to her lips and then kept reading. When she'd finished, Shay carried first one boy and then the other to their room. Although they settled into cribs, they'd refused to sleep apart. He tor, night-light and music box. Tiptoeing out of the room, he closed the door behind him. *What a day.*

In the kitchen, Mom stood at the counter, ladling beef stew onto a plate. "Have you had supper?"

He shook his head. "No. The boys did, but I didn't get a chance."

"I'll warm this up. Would you like some bread? I brought rolls."

"You didn't have to do all that. What's Dad eating?"

She waved him off. "I'm happy to help. You need to eat, son."

His mouth watered. In the weeks after Monica's sudden departure, the anger and confusion were all-consuming. People brought meals, but most of it ended up in the garbage. Now, almost a year later, he craved real food again. He could sit at the table with the boys and not let the empty fourth chair bring him to tears.

Mom slid the plate into the microwave.

"You didn't answer my question. Where's Dad tonight?"

While his supper reheated, she took a glass from

the cupboard and filled it with ice and water. He waited. The set of her shoulders indicated she didn't want to talk about it. But they never talked about it. That was the problem.

"He has plenty to eat. Don't worry about hire

"Mom, if you coming here is an is—a nanny."

The microwave beeped. Don't be silly. I love coming over."

"But Dad doesn't."

She pressed her lips into a thin line and carried his plate to the table.

He followed, gently placing his hand on her arm. "I'm serious. I hired help in Virginia, and I can do it again here."

"Nonsense. You don't need strangers watching the boys. That's what grandmothers are for."

"Not when it aggravates the grandpa."

She offered a sad smile. "Don't you worry about your father. I trailed him all over creation for years with the military. This is how I want to spend my retirement. He understands."

"But he doesn't have any time for his only grandchildren." Shay bowed his head and silently thanked God for his food. When he opened his eyes, Mom stared at the table, cupping her glass of water with both hands.

"He loves Aiden and Liam in his own way." Her voice, thick with emotion, gave him pause.

Measuring his words, Shay spread a paper napkin across his lap. "At some point, he's got to demonstrate that. They're perceptive. They'll start asking why Grandpa never wants to hang out with them."

"Honey, we aren't going to change your father. The best thing we can do is keep praying and creating opportunities for him to be involved."

Shay speared a bite of meat with his fork. While her response carried truth and wisdom, it still stung. So far, Dad had avoided almost all interaction with the boys. He'd come by the house once, maybe twice, since they'd moved in. The complex web of hurt and guilt undergirding most of his interactions with his father wasn't the boys' fault. He wouldn't let them carry the heavy burden of disapproval.

"Were you able to join that committee the young lady at the birthday party mentioned?"

Shay dipped his bread in the broth, pooling on his plate, too hungry to protest her deliberate shift to a new topic. "Yes. My first meeting was this afternoon."

"Oh? How'd it go?"

"Great. Looks like the fire department will play a big role in the festival."

"Wonderful. I'm sure you'll be a tremendous help."

"Hope so." He also hoped he could find a way to get Natalie's teasing smile out of his head. His thoughts had turned to her often. Too often. Dating wasn't even an option. They'd lost so much when Monica left. While the thought of being a single dad forever planted an icy ball in his gut, bringing someone new into the boys' lives was a risk he wasn't willing to take.

Chapter Three

By the middle of the week, Natalie's stomach was twisted in knots over the email from Forever Love, as well as the lack of progress on the service project. She paced the street in front of the unfinished house, her mind racing. Discarded candy wrappers and empty plastic water bottles littered the quiet space. Despite the community's faithful commitment to help, they were woefully behind. At this rate, they'd have little more than a shelter to offer their chosen family.

She stopped pacing and glanced across the street to her family's farm. Even though she'd read Karen's email at least a dozen times, she still couldn't believe it was real. The thought of telling her parents about the offer had squelched her initial enthusiasm. She'd conveniently avoided the conversation and kept the offer a secret from everyone. Maybe she needed to just get it over with. She fished her phone from the back pocket of her jeans and mentally rehearsed the call.

Hey, Mama. Got a minute? I'm thinking about selling Magnolia Lane and moving to...

Ha. That would not go over well. She sighed and shoved her phone back in her pocket. This was home. All she'd ever known, minus her years spent an hour away in Chapel Hill, at the university. Could she pick up and start over in Charlotte? If she said no, would she always wonder *what if*?

The uncertainty weighed heavily on her mind. Despite her own personal heartache, orchestrating weddings that exceeded brides' expectations made her happy. Fulfilled. Their ecstatic smiles, and the groom's expression when he saw his bride for the first time, made all her efforts behind the scenes worth it. Forever Love's offer meant an end to juggling Magnolia Lane and the farm. An end to her constant frustration over turning away clients because she felt pulled in two directions. She'd always dreamed of planning weddings full-time. Was this finally her chance to pursue her dream?

Tires crunched on gravel behind her, and she turned around. Three pickup trucks had turned off the highway and approached, easing into a tight line on one side of the street.

Car doors slammed, and she counted six men reaching into truck beds and pulling out toolboxes, power saws and a portable cooler. The guy parked closest to her was the last one to get out of his truck.

When his boots hit the ground, he grinned at her through the driver's-side window.

Her pulse kicked up a notch. *Shay?*

The guys chatted back and forth while they hauled their tools and supplies toward her. She stared in disbelief.

"Hey, Natalie," Shay called out, pausing to anchor his tool belt around his waist. "How's it going?"

"I'm—you—why are y'all here?" Warmth flooded her cheeks as she struggled to form a coherent sentence.

"Campbell rounded us up." Trent angled his head toward Shay. "He said you needed a little help finishing this house."

"A little help?" She let out a wan laugh. "That's an understatement."

Shay grabbed a large bottle of water from the truck's cab. "We're prepared to work hard. Why don't you give us a quick rundown. What needs to be done first?"

The guys—most of them familiar faces from around town—fanned out around her, waiting expectantly.

"I—I don't even know where to start. There's so much to do. Finishing the plumbing and electrical work, hanging the drywall…"

"I'm up for a challenge. How about y'all?" Trent shifted his toolbox to his other hand and motioned for the guys to follow him.

They made their way up the driveway and onto

the crude front steps, their work boots clunking against the plywood.

Shay stepped away, but she reached out and touched his arm. "Wait."

His gaze traveled slowly from her fingers to her face. When their eyes met, something passed between them—an unmistakable spark that made her mouth dry and tangled her thoughts. Again.

Shay raised an eyebrow. "Something on your mind?"

She dropped her hand to her side before it lingered a second longer. "Thank you. Really. You have no idea how much this means to me."

"You're welcome."

"What can I do to help you? Who's watching your kids? I mean, I'm assuming you're single and all. Otherwise…" She pressed her lips together, heat climbing up her neck. *Just stop talking.*

His eyes gleamed, and a smile tugged at his lips. "Why do you ask? Is there childcare included for frequent visitors to the pumpkin patch?"

"Very funny. No, I'm not offering childcare." She stopped short of mentioning that he probably wouldn't trust her with his boys, given her limited experience with the toddler crowd.

"The boys are napping. I took a walk on the wild side and hired a babysitter since my mom's enjoying a day off."

"Good for you. I hear there are a few reliable ones around."

He checked his phone. "So far, so good. She hasn't called me."

"They're sleeping, right? How much trouble could they get into?"

Shay chuckled. "You don't have kids, do you?"

"No." She shook her head. "Can't you tell?"

He studied her, as though he was going to say more. Instead, he put his phone away and grabbed his water. "I better get to work."

"I didn't bring any tools over, but if you have an extra hammer, I'd be glad to help out for a little bit."

His eyes widened. "Seriously?"

She fisted her hands on her hips. "What? Girls aren't allowed to use hammers?"

"I didn't say that."

"You didn't have to. Your expression said it all."

"I'm pretty sure we can round up an extra hammer."

"Good. Tell the guys supper's on me. I'll run and grab something when y'all get hungry."

A wide smile stretched across his face, rocketing her heart rate into orbit. "Deal."

Shay lingered in the driveway, feeling like a teenager with that stupid grin plastered across his face. He needed to get inside and get to work. The jolt of electricity that zinged from Natalie's fingertips to his arm was hard to ignore. So was a pretty girl with the courage to grab a hammer and help build a house. Annoyed that he found the idea so appealing, his smile faded, and he reached for his tools.

"Shay? Do you have a tape measure on you? I must've left mine at home."

Shay pivoted. Trent stood in the open doorway, one hand braced on the frame. His gaze flitted toward Natalie and then back to Shay. Curiosity flickered in his expression, and Shay willed him not to say a word. *Nothing to see here.*

"Yep." Shay unclipped his tape measure from his tool belt and met Trent at the top of the steps. "Where should I start?"

"We've got to finish the subflooring first. Natalie, you're going to have to get somebody else in here to handle the electrical stuff."

"Yeah, I know." Gravel crunched under her feet as she strode up behind Shay. "Electricians who are available to wire a whole house are hard to come by around here. Is there something else I can help with?"

Trent's mouth twitched. "I don't want to offend you, but we don't expect you to move sheets of plywood by yourself."

Natalie laughed, brushing past him and into the house. "I'm not offended. I didn't want to move plywood, anyway."

Shay stepped inside and studied the layout. The entry opened to a kitchen and breakfast nook on one side and a living area on the other. What would eventually be a hallway led to the bedrooms.

Through the unfinished walls, he counted three more rooms, a bathroom and laundry area.

"How would you feel about operating a glue gun?" Shay asked.

Natalie faced him. "A glue gun? For what?"

"If we glue the subflooring to the joists, it keeps the floors from squeaking."

Trent shot him a look. "You've obviously done this before."

He shrugged. "Maybe a few times."

"If you're not careful, Natalie will appoint you project manager," Trent said.

"No kidding." Natalie smiled up at Shay. "If you tell me you were an electrician in a former life, I might hug you."

Promise? Heat crept up his neck. An awkward pause ensued. "I'm afraid you'll have to settle for hugging a glue gun instead."

Trent smothered a laugh with a cough and turned away.

Natalie rolled her eyes. "Aren't you clever. Show me this glue gun, and we'll get started."

"Sweet. Let's look back here." He crossed to the hallway and stopped in the opening for the first bedroom. Sheets of plywood leaned against the far wall in a neat stack. A glue gun and several boxes of nails were balanced on top of an overturned bucket.

Natalie came up behind him. "Did you find—"

He held out a hand to keep her from coming any

farther. "Watch your step. It looks like whoever started the installation stopped right about here."

The fragrance of her perfume—sweet and flowery—teased his senses as she pulled her hair into a ponytail and secured it with a band she'd slid from her wrist. There wasn't anywhere for him to go. She had the only exit blocked, and the exposed floor joists kept him from moving farther into the room. But he didn't trust himself to stand there, feeling the sleeve of her plaid shirt brush against his arm, while he figured out how to play it cool and put them both to work.

"Trent, why don't you and I lay down a few boards first? That will give Natalie a surface to stand or kneel on while she adheres the glue."

"You got it." Trent lingered behind Natalie, unable to squeeze past her.

"You don't have to make a place for me to stand." She looked around the room. "I can balance on the floor thingies—what are they called again?"

"Joists." Trent and Shay spoke in unison.

Shay walked carefully across the narrow boards, toward the stack of plywood. "Stay where you are until Trent and I get things set up."

"But what about the glue?" She reached for the gun. "I thought you said this went down first?"

Shay paused. "You don't take no for an answer, do you?"

She grinned. "Not usually."

"Fine. Come over here, and I'll show you how to

get started. Trent, if you'll help me move this plywood, we'll slide it right in behind her."

Natalie proved to be a quick learner. He thought
he'd spend a lot of extra time coaching her and
waiting for her to maneuver in the small space. But
she surprised him by working efficiently. It wasn't
long before they had half the room finished.

"Isn't there a chalk line or something we're supposed to draw?" She leaned back on her heels, resting on a fresh sheet of plywood.

Shay exchanged glances with Trent. "How did
you know that?"

"I googled installing a subfloor last night."

"Were you planning to do this yourself?"

Natalie brushed a strand of hair from her eyes.
"If I had to."

"I don't have a chalk line with me." Shay opened
a box of nails, biting back a smile. She was really
something. He pretended to fumble around, looking for his hammer—anything to distract him from
admiring the way her pink lips quirked to one side
as she surveyed their progress.

"That's one thing I did remember." Trent stood
and rummaged in his toolbox.

Natalie hummed softly while they waited. Shay
had forgotten what it was like to have a woman
around, singing while she worked. He looked away.
Despite his best efforts, memories of married life
popped up when he least expected.

"Found it." Trent held the chalk line in his hand.

"Excellent. If you'll hold one end, I'll grab the other and we can snap these lines." Shay got back to work with a renewed focus. This project mattered. A home for a veteran and his family mattered. He'd help however he could. If it meant working side by side with a certain farmer's daughter, then he'd have to make sure they never worked alone.

Chapter Four

Natalie massaged her aching back. In her brief history as Magnolia Lane's owner, she'd glued hundreds of bows on party favors and re-strung dozens of white twinkle lights in the barn, but none of that compared to the fatigue she felt from being hunched over, squirting glue on narrow pieces of wood.

Shay and Trent kept going, though, so she would, too. After she'd finished spreading the glue, she'd taken over snapping the chalk lines so Trent and Shay could nail down the floorboards. She wasn't a stranger to swinging a hammer, but they definitely worked faster than she did.

Long shadows fell across the wood they'd installed. The reddish-orange glow of late afternoon sunlight reminded her she still had plenty to do today—and it didn't involve spending quality time next to Shay Campbell. Even though she'd vowed to quit, she'd caught herself staring at him more than once, especially when he tossed his windbreaker aside and revealed yet another snug-fitting T-shirt. Every time he moved another sheet of plywood, her gaze was drawn to his muscles rippling beneath the faded fabric.

She saw Trent look at his watch. "Do you need to go?"

"Yeah, I should. Caroline will want to feed the girls supper pretty soon."

Natalie palmed her forehead. "I was going to bring you guys something to eat."

"We'll be back to help you again." Trent packed up his tools. "You can feed us some other time."

"But I offered—"

"I can't speak for Shay, but I'll have to take a rain check. Something was already cooking in the Crock-Pot before I left the house. Caroline will not be happy if I'm not there to eat it." Trent shrugged into the faded plaid button-down he'd discarded earlier.

"I understand." She sneaked another quick look at Shay. He pressed his lips into a thin line while he cleaned up his work space. He hadn't declined her offer for a meal, but he wasn't expressing much interest, either.

She hung back, staying out of the way while they packed up and headed outside to their trucks. The other guys who'd come with them had left already.

"Thank you, Trent." She gave her friend's husband a side hug. "Please tell Caroline and the girls how much I appreciate them giving up an after-noon with you."

Trent grinned, squeezing her shoulder. "No prob-lem. I'll try to round up some more help, especially an electrician."

"Yes. I'm desperately seeking an electrician. If he can recommend a great plumber, that would be sweet, too."

"I'll see what I can do." Trent climbed into his truck and waved at them through the open window. "See y'all later."

Shay gave his friend a casual salute. "Have a good night."

After Trent drove off, Natalie turned and faced Shay. "Thank you, again. Are you sure I can't feed you? The boys are welcome to come over to The Grille for cheeseburgers, too. Or…"

His pained expression caused her to trail off.

"What? What did I say? You look like I kicked you in the teeth."

He lowered his tool belt to the ground and jammed his hands in his back pockets.

"I'm not very good at taking the boys out by my-self." His voice strained, he scuffed the toe of his work boot against the ground.

Her heart climbed into her throat. "Oh."

"Germs, food allergy issues, the stress of han-dling two little kids in public… I can't seem to—"

"Shay, it's fine. I get it. Not a big deal."

He held up a hand. "Please, let me finish. Selfishly, I'd like to have supper with you tonight. But it's chaotic and messy and very little adult conversation will take place."

Talk about mixed signals. "Is that an invitation? I'm confused."

Sighing, he scrubbed a hand across the stubble clinging to his jaw.

Her eyes trailed his fingertips, sending her thoughts places they shouldn't go.

"What I'm trying to say is that evenings with the boys are a struggle. Throw in a meal in a public place and we're a disaster waiting to happen."

"Why don't we order pizza and eat with the boys? If you're okay with that." She wanted to clamp her hand over her mouth. Or disappear. *Listen to you, inviting yourself to his place.*

He mulled it over. "Are you sure you're up for it?"

"I'm not afraid of two little boys. How bad could it be?"

"Consider yourself warned." The corners of his mouth twitched.

Sliding her phone from her pocket, she pulled up the number for the only local pizza restaurant. "If I order it now, we could swing by and pick it up on the way."

Shay hesitated, hovering near the bed of his truck.

She winced. Yep, way too direct. He was probably conjuring up an excuse right this minute.

Shay put his tools away and then circled around to meet her on the passenger side. "I'm going to have to ask you to drive yourself and pick up the pizza. I've got to get home. I'm already running late."

"Right. Absolutely."

"I wouldn't be able to drive you home, anyway. The boys will need to go to bed, and I can't leave them." He reached over and opened the door for her. "Why don't I give you a ride to your car?"

"Sure. It's over at the farm." She slid into the passenger seat without looking at him, warmth flushing her skin. Could she be any more insensitive to his situation? Of course he couldn't hang out, lingering around the table and enjoying meaningful conversation. The boys needed him. Depended on him. She only wanted to thank him for helping with the house and giving up precious time with his boys. It wasn't like she had ulterior motives. A serious relationship with a firefighter wasn't an option. The agony of Spencer's passing had taught her to guard her heart. Shay was a teammate, who was striving for a common goal. Nothing more.

Thirty minutes later, Shay dragged a damp cloth across the kitchen table, scrubbing at some honey or jelly or other mysterious sticky substance that refused to budge. Liam and Aiden toddled around in circles, babbling at one another.

A sea of toys spread from one side of the living

room to the other. The babysitter had said they'd only been awake for an hour before he got home. So how had they managed to make such a huge mess? He'd had everything picked up before he left to work on the house.

Satisfied with the condition of the table, he turned and tossed the rag into the sink. Aiden cruised into Shay's path, his chubby bare feet thumping against the floor.

"Hey, buddy." Shay patted his head then scooted by, checking the clock on his way to the pantry to grab more napkins. Natalie would probably be here soon. It couldn't take long to order a pizza in Meadow Springs. Someone's blanket lay in the middle of the floor. He leaned down and scooped it up, draping it over his shoulder as he opened the pantry door. She'd definitely get to see the realities of life with small children.

Doubt pinged through him. What was he doing letting her come over? Yes, she'd offered. But he could've declined. Hadn't he vowed not to be alone with her? In reality, he didn't want to be alone with the boys tonight. A wave of guilt rushed in. How messed up was that? Napkins in hand, he closed the pantry door and leaned his forehead against it, squeezing his eyes shut.

"Da-da?" Liam called out. Tiny fingers tugged at Shay's pant leg, reminding him of his first priority.

Shay opened his eyes and glanced down. Liam's wide-cyed stare made his heart expand. He looped the blanket around Liam's neck, earning an adorable belly laugh. He surveyed the kitchen one more time. Breakfast and lunch dishes still sat on the counter, next to an empty casserole pan from last night. With a heavy sigh, he turned away. Welcoming Natalie into his world was a bad idea. The boys weren't ready. He wasn't ready. His heart, much like his new home, was still in pieces.

A light knock sounded on the door. Too late. Couldn't back out now.

Aiden beat him there. Standing on tiptoe, he strained to reach the doorknob.

"Hold on. It's locked." Shay tucked the napkins under his arm and then turned the dead bolt and swung the door open.

Natalie stood on the porch, holding a large pizza box, her smile chipping away at his concerns. *Two friends sharing a pizza. That's all.*

"What's going on, fellas?"

"Come on in." Shay stepped back, and Natalie came inside. "Aiden, Liam, this is Miss Natalie. Can you say hello?"

"Eat? Eat?" Liam's gaze flitted between Shay, Natalie and the pizza box.

Shay chuckled. "Yes. We're having pizza. Let's sit down, please."

Aiden and Liam turned and scrambled toward their booster seats strapped to the kitchen chairs, dancing impatiently for someone to help them.

Natalie stared after them. "I've never seen toddlers move so fast."

"I think they might be hungry. Here, let me put that on the counter." He reached for the box, his fingers brushing against hers. Warmth flooded through him as her gaze locked with his.

"Is there anything I can do to help?"

He lingered, drinking in the sight of her pink cheeks and tendrils from her ponytail framing her face. How had he not noticed earlier that her shirt made her eyes seem bluer somehow?

"Drinks? Plates?" she prompted him.

"Oh. Yeah. Sure." He dragged his gaze away and angled his head toward the kitchen. "Cups and plates are in the cabinets above the sink. Please excuse the mess."

"No judgment here. I can't keep up with my own chores, and there's only one of me."

"Daddy, help."

Shay abandoned the pizza on the counter and crossed to the table, where the boys struggled to get seated.

"Please? Please?" Liam patted his palm against his chest.

"I know, I'm hungry, too. Give us a minute." Shay clicked Liam's belt, securing him into his booster seat.

"Are these okay?" Natalie held up two smaller plates with popular cartoon characters painted on them.

"Mine," Aiden squealed, stretching both arms toward her.

"No, no." Liam's eyes filled with tears.

Shay groaned inside. He'd tried to hide those plates at least twice since he unpacked the kitchen. Mom must have brought them back out. For whatever reason, the boys fought like crazy over who used the red instead of the orange. But he didn't have the heart to correct Natalie. She was only trying to help.

"I guess that's a yes." She set both plates on the counter. "How about drinks?"

"The boys will have milk." Shay filled two glasses with ice from the dispenser on the refrigerator door. "The options for grown-ups are limited, I'm afraid. Water, sweet tea…there might be a diet soda in here somewhere."

"Water's fine. Thank you." Natalie opened the lid and reached for a slice of pizza.

Shay hesitated, tempted to prompt her to wash her hands. He hated to say something. But he couldn't risk the boys getting sick or—worse— triggering an allergic reaction.

She stepped away. "Mind if I wash my hands first?"

"Not at all. There's a restroom in the hallway." He gestured toward the open door and then carried their water to the table. Aiden and Liam were starting to whine. "We're coming. Hang in there."

He worked quickly, cutting cheese pizza into smaller bites for the boys, before mutiny erupted.

When Natalie returned, Shay had a plate waiting for her.

She slid into the extra chair at the table. "Can I get the boys their milk?"

"My cup, my cup." Liam's face crumpled as he scanned the kitchen, no doubt searching for his preferred sippy cup.

Shay sighed, longing to relax and eat the pizza, which was growing colder by the second.

"Let me." Natalie stood again. "I can get it, if you'll—"

"No." He stood, his chair scraping against the floor and his voice a little too gruff. "It's easier if I do it."

She froze. "Oh."

An awkward silence blanketed the kitchen. He winced, striding toward the refrigerator and mentally kicking himself for being such a control freak. It wasn't rocket science. She was more than capable of completing the task.

The boys—normally jabbering through the whole meal—were very quiet. They must've sensed the tension. He poured milk into the blue sippy cup for Liam and the green for Aiden, twisted the tops on and delivered them to the table.

Natalie sat in her seat, staring at her plate.

Shay sat down and offered his hand. She regarded it tentatively, confusion clouding her features.

"I'm sorry. That was rude. You offered to help and I didn't let you do anything."

She pressed her hand against his. "It's okay. I'm sure you have your own way of doing things."

"Thank you for being so gracious. I've had to apologize a lot lately for my actions."

Natalie arched an eyebrow.

"Maybe I should say the blessing." He bowed his head. "Lord, thank You for providing for our needs and for a productive day working on the house. Amen."

"Amen," the boys mumbled around mouths full of pizza.

She chuckled. "They're adorable."

Shay shook his head. "I'm glad you think so. Table manners aren't their strong suit." Reluctantly, he let go of Natalie's hand and reached for his pizza. "Half meat and half cheese. How did you know that's what we liked?"

"Trent and Caroline's girls only eat cheese pizza. I figured you probably preferred something more manly. I'm glad I got it right." She smiled again and spread a napkin across her lap.

His pulse quickened at the gleam in her eye. He averted his gaze. *Just friends…sharing a pizza.* "So what else is going on besides this house project? Are you expecting a big crowd at the farm this weekend?"

"I hope so. This month is usually our best, except for the first weekend in December."

"December? Aren't the pumpkins gone by then?"

"Yes, but we transform the farm into a festival of Christmas lights and offer hot chocolate with the hay rides. It's a huge hit."

"Wow. Sounds impressive."

"We think so. It's my favorite season."

His stomach tightened. December was hardly his favorite anymore.

As if reading his thoughts, she offered a sympathetic glance. "I can imagine the holidays look and feel a lot different for you now."

"For sure." He stared down at his half-eaten slice of pizza. "Never imagined I'd be going it alone."

"If you don't mind my asking—"

"She left." His gaze met hers. The sour tone in his voice drew a worried gaze from both Liam and Aiden. He softened the rest of his response. "Professional singing had always been on her radar. She must've found an opportunity too good to pass up. Apparently, putting her dreams on hold for us wasn't an option."

Natalie's eyes widened. "I—I'm sorry. That must've been very difficult."

"Extremely." He glanced at the boys again and forced a smile. "It's all right. Campbell men are resilient. Lesson learned. With God's help, we're moving forward."

"More? More?" Liam pushed his empty plate across the table.

"Sure, buddy." He stood up, grateful for the distraction. He didn't want to talk about Monica tonight, especially in front of the boys. They were far too young to understand. Besides, he and Natalie were barely more than acquaintances. No need to delve deeper. Despite her empathetic expression, which invited him to share more, he wouldn't. He couldn't. Openness and vulnerability implied a relationship. It would be wrong to lead her on and pretend that a relationship was a possibility, no matter how much he enjoyed her company.

Chapter Five

On Saturday evening, Natalie slipped out the back door of the barn at Magnolia Lane. The bride and groom drove away only moments before, and the DJ had just finished playing the last song. She sank into an Adirondack chair and tipped her head back, with a plastic cup of fruit-infused water in her hand, and admired the beautiful moon and stars twinkling down from an inky black sky.

"Another happily-ever-after," she whispered in the semidarkness, a twinge of sadness pricking at her. No matter how many times she pulled off a flawless reception, the reminder of what might've been hovered just beneath the surface. Especially tonight. Spencer had made her laugh and brought her flowers he'd picked from the side of the road. And he could charm her mother in a second. They'd made plans for a future together. But she'd worried every time he told her about sprinting into a life-threatening situation. The anxiety clawing at her insides when he was on shift had felt unbearable sometimes. Seeing his parents near the buffet line tonight set an ache in her chest and provoked mental images of everything they'd lost that night.

She heaved a sigh and took a sip of her water. No sense longing for what might have been. Her thoughts shifted to the offer from Forever Love. Her meeting with Karen was only five days away. She needed to make a decision before they spoke on the phone Thursday. Based on some quick research, the terms seemed fair. The benefits and compensation were generous, too. Maybe a fresh start in Charlotte was exactly what she needed. She still hadn't broached the subject with Mama and Daddy, though. The idea planted an icy ball of dread in her stomach.

A tentative prayer for wisdom formed in her mind, but she quickly snuffed it out. God hadn't granted a lot of clarity lately. Why would this scenario be any different?

Shadows moving near the back fence captured her attention. Guests wandering away from the reception? It wouldn't be the first time. Except this was one person, and he didn't look like he'd dressed to attend a wedding. She squinted, trying to get a better view in the glow of the lights spilling from the barn's open back door.

"Natalie?" Shay called out, moving closer.

"Hey. I didn't recognize you. What are you doing, lurking along the back fence?"

"I hope I didn't startle you." He stepped into the light, his face glistening with sweat. "I was out for a run and saw the lights, thought I'd see... I guess I'm sort of crashing somebody's party, aren't I?"

"It's almost over." She nudged the extra chair beside her with her foot. "Have a seat."

He mopped the moisture from his temple with the hem of his T-shirt, giving Natalie a glimpse of his chiseled abs. *Mercy.* She chugged another long sip of water.

"I'm not exactly wearing formal party attire." Shay sank into the chair.

She set her empty cup on the ground. "We won't kick you out."

"Natalie, would you like some—" Bridget, one of her part-time employees, came outside, carrying a small tray loaded with slices of cake; she stopped when her gaze landed on Shay "—cake?"

Natalie stifled a laugh at Bridget's expression. It was probably the first time she'd walked out that door and nearly dumped four slices of wedding cake in the lap of a handsome stranger. "Sure, we'd love some cake."

"Um, okay." Bridget lowered the tray to a discarded wooden crate they kept nearby for late-night leftover consumption.

"Bridget, this is my...new friend, Shay. He works for the fire department. Shay, this is Bridget."

Shay stood and extended his hand. "It's nice to meet you, Bridget."

"You, too." Bridget wiped her hands on her apron, quickly shook his hand and then disappeared back inside.

"I think I scared her." Shay sat back down.

"Only a little. She'll recover. Here, have some cake." Natalie slid a plate off the tray. "Why are you running late at night by yourself?"

He picked up a plate and carved the fork through the end of a slice. "My mom stayed over tonight. Dad's on a fishing trip with some buddies, and she didn't want to be alone."

"So she's with the boys while you work out? That's nice of her."

"I need all the help I can get. Plus, I like to work out."

"I noticed."

He paused, a forkful of cake halfway to his mouth.

Warmth flamed her face. *Oh. My.* Was that out loud? She crammed a bite of cake into her mouth and avoided eye contact. Maybe he didn't hear her.

Shay grinned. "I'll take that as a compliment."

The cake clogged her dry throat. If only she hadn't drained her water moments before.

"I wanted to run something by you, an idea I had for the house."

Natalie managed to find her voice. "Sure, let's hear it."

"There's a woman who runs a parents' morning out program at the community center… Janeanne?

I stopped by to register the boys, and she mentioned her cousin's an electrician. Do you know him?"

"Robert? I'd heard he was back in town. Is he willing to help us out?"

"Maybe. I thought I'd better ask you before—"

Bridget poked her head out the door. "You can come back inside whenever you're ready. The coast is clear."

"Thanks. I'll be there in a few."

Shay arched an eyebrow. "An unwanted guest?"

"My former boyfriend's parents were here."

"Ouch." He grimaced. "Is that why you're hiding out here?"

She froze. "Not exactly. Spencer and I...haven't been together for a while." That was a true statement, without blurting all the details. Goose bumps pebbled her flesh. While the other firefighters around town knew about what happened, they never brought it up. The occasional sympathetic glance was all she got when they came in The Grille now.

"Is there more to the story?"

Her breath caught in her throat. This was harder than she had expected. "He was a firefighter," she whispered. "At a station in Raleigh. One night, they were called to a fire at an apartment complex, and he—he didn't make it out."

Shay's complexion paled. "I'm so sorry. Man, I hate to hear that."

"Thank you. Spencer was a great guy. It was

heartbreaking for all of us. But he's been gone two years. I should be able to speak to his mama without having a meltdown." She offered an apologetic smile. "Sorry. This is probably more drama than you anticipated."

Something undecipherable flickered in his eyes. "It's not dramatic. I'd have a hard time speaking to my ex-wife's parents if I ran into them."

She stopped short of asking him more about his ex-wife. The few details he'd shared the other night had replayed in her mind, particularly his obvious hurt over a woman pursuing a dream at the expense of her marriage. Ouch. He was a firefighter, and she was a dreamer with a fantastic opportunity. That pretty much put a damper on the attraction sparking between them. Changing the subject was safer. "How long will your dad be away on his fishing trip?"

He shrugged, chewing slowly.

"Where did he go? The beach?"

Shay swallowed, his face a mask of indifference. "I'm not sure. We don't communicate well. Never have."

"Sounds complicated."

"Not really. He was busy with his military career, and I pretty much grew up in a boarding school."

"You're kidding."

"About which part?"

"How long did you go to boarding school?"

"From fourth grade on. My dad received orders

to go overseas and thought it would be best if I stayed in Virginia."

"Do you have any siblings?"

He hesitated. "Not anymore. My brother drowned. The summer before fourth grade."

"I don't even know what to say." She reached out and touched his arm, her heart aching. "That must've been tough."

"Thank you. We've never fully recovered as a family. I—I'm not sure I'll ever stop feeling guilty."

"Why do you feel guilty?"

Pain twisted his expression. "I would've done a lot of things different that day."

She withdrew her hand, conscious of the warmth flowing from his skin, and smoothed her skirt over her knees. "Did you see your parents very often?"

"Twice a year when they were overseas. A little more often when they came back to the States. My grandparents lived close to the boarding school, so I spent my vacations with them. It wasn't so bad. Nothing like what you've seen in the movies. I made some great friends who are like brothers."

"It sounds like you made the most of a hard situation."

"How about you? Ever lived anywhere else?"

"Besides college? No."

"You're fortunate. Not many people have what you have—a family business keeping them all together, reenforcing a strong heritage, deepening those roots." He leaned forward and set his empty plate on the ground. "That's something I'd love to give my boys."

"You make it sound so picture-perfect."

"Are you saying it's not?"

"There's pros and cons." She shifted in her chair. "Working with family is rewarding, but it's also a challenge. We know how to push each other's buttons, the balance of power is often unequal, there's endless debate about implementing change. I could go on and on."

"Have you considered other options?"

She bit her lip. "Funny you should ask. An unexpected opportunity just developed, but I'm worried my family won't be receptive to change."

"There's that endless debate thing, right?"

"You have no idea." She stopped short of revealing her own role in the dilemma. They were just friends. Teammates with a shared mission, right? Isn't that what she'd decided? She'd already told him about Spencer—no need to overshare. Even if she didn't accept the position with Forever Love and sell Magnolia Lane, a relationship with a firefighter was out of the question.

The girl who'd fled earlier reappeared, hovering in the doorway of the barn. "Natalie? Is there anything else you need? The guests are gone."

Natalie stood up. "No, I have to come in tomorrow, so I'll finish cleaning up then. Thanks,

Bridget." She quickly hugged the slender young woman. "Great job tonight."

Bridget gave a shy smile. "Thanks. G'night."

Shay stood, wishing their conversation didn't have to end. "Is there anything I could help you with so you don't have to clean up tomorrow?"

Natalie frowned. "Don't you want to go home?"

"No. Mom and the boys are sleeping, and I'd rather not face that giant stack of boxes sitting in my garage."

"If you're sure."

"Depends what you ask me to do."

She laughed and turned to go inside. "I'll put you in charge of folding all the tablecloths."

He stayed rooted in place. "On second thought—"

Whirling around, she flashed a grin that made his pulse skitter.

"I'm kidding. No folding required. We have to send them to the cleaners."

"Sounds easy enough." He stepped through the doorway and surveyed the room. Round tables dotted wide-planked, rustic pine floors. The far side of the room sat bare and empty, except for large speakers and a guy he presumed to be the DJ, who was hauling his equipment toward the front entrance. Overhead, exposed wood beams decorated with strands of old-fashioned globe lights supported the vaulted ceiling. "Wow. This is impressive."

Natalie weaved her way among the tables, gathering glass jars holding fresh flowers. "Have you not been here before?"

"Nope. Did you restore this yourself?" He followed her around, grabbing more of the flower arrangements from surrounding tables.

"I had some help." She angled her head toward the brick wall. "This used to be a livery. These are the original walls. I had the floors restored, and the kitchen is new and up to code, of course."

"How many events a year do you host?"

"This year, I have seventy-five bookings."

He let out a low whistle. "That's at least one a week."

"I'd do more if I didn't manage the farm, too. In a perfect world, I'd just do weddings and receptions, but for now, I'll handle almost any type of event."

"Have you considered finding a way to devote more time to wedding planning?"

"Maybe." Natalie passed him an empty garbage bag, clearly unwilling to elaborate. "We'd better get to work, or we'll be here all night. It's not glamorous, but if you could pick up any garbage left behind and toss it in here, I'd appreciate it."

"Not a problem." He moved quickly through the spacious room, dropping used napkins and abandoned cups into the bag. As he cleaned up, he wondered how Natalie even managed to juggle both of her responsibilities. Judging by the way her eyes lit up when she talked about this space, it was clear she felt both content and confident. And she'd obviously built a name for herself, given the barn's popularity. No wonder she enjoyed event planning—it was definitely her gift.

"Wow, keep up this pace, and I'll put you on the payroll." Natalie came behind him, tugging the cloths from the tables.

"Ha. You're funny. I've got enough work for now, thank you."

"True. Thanks for helping. Hopefully now I can spend a couple of hours working on the house after church."

He tied the drawstrings on the bag, this tidbit of info motivating him to look forward to Sunday, too. "Once the boys are down for their naps, I thought I'd swing by the house and see what I could do."

"Sweet." She added another tablecloth to the bundle in her arms. "A few of the guys came by this week and finished the subfloor."

"That's awesome."

"The windows should be here soon, too."

"Do you think that puts you on track to get the house finished in time?"

"I doubt it. The paint, finishing touches, interior decorating—all that will take a while, and we've only got a month left."

"They make it look so easy on those TV shows, don't they?"

Her eyes widened. "A firefighter who watches home-decorating shows? I can't believe it."

He pressed his finger to his lips. "Don't let that

get out, all right? The guys at the station would have a hay day."

She smirked. "They certainly would. No worries. Your secret is safe with me."

He bit the inside of his cheek. If only he could trust her with more. Something about her made him want to tell her everything. Flustered, he hauled the garbage bag outside to the trash cans he'd seen near the back door. Moonlight spilled onto the cobblestones at his feet. He shivered in the cool air, wishing he'd grabbed a sweatshirt or windbreaker before he'd left his house.

Natalie joined him a few minutes later, her keys jangling as she locked the door. "We're all finished. Thanks again for your help."

"You're welcome." He looked down the empty tree-lined drive. "Did you walk here?"

"Of course. I have my own place on the farm, not too far from the gazebo."

"But it's so late."

"Afraid I'll turn into a pumpkin?" Her voice held a teasing note.

"No. I'm not comfortable letting you walk home alone in the dark."

"I've lived here my whole life. I'm the one that should be concerned about you. How were you planning to get back? Jump the fence?"

Scraping his knuckles along his jaw, he realized she was probably right. He'd intruded on her turf and then found excuses to stick around. Now he was fussing at her for taking a walk she could likely navigate in her sleep. Although the line dividing her property from his neighborhood wasn't far away, he had no idea how to get home if he walked her back to her place.

Natalie chuckled. "I'll tell you what. Let's walk over to where my car is parked in the lot beside The Grille, and I'll give you a ride home."

"Fair enough." He waited while she double-checked the locks on the doors.

"I'll rest easier knowing you aren't cavorting through my pumpkin patch in the dark, looking for a short cut."

"Cavorting, huh? That's a fancy word."

"I'm a sophisticated farmer's daughter." She rummaged in her bag and then pulled out a flashlight that had probably been around for a couple of decades. "Although, I'm kicking it old school with my vintage light."

"There's an app for that, you know."

"You sound like my sisters."

They left the courtyard and started down the winding gravel path from the barn, walking in companionable silence until they reached the corn maze.

"Oh, look." He eyed the entrance. "Isn't this where you almost forced me to deliver a baby?"

She turned and swatted his upper arm. "I think you're confused. This is where you tried your best to make Maria give birth in a golf cart."

He rubbed his bicep and faked a grimace. "If

it weren't for me, she would've never made it to that ambulance."

"Oh, please. I was the one driving the golf cart. Besides, I thought we already established my emergency plan was spot on?"

"I'm teasing." Reaching over, he tugged on a lock of her hair. He was unprepared for the way the silky strands would feel against his fingers, or the sensations unfurling in his abdomen. It had been a long time since he'd touched a woman, much less stroked her hair.

Natalie stopped walking and looked up at him, the glow from the flashlight illuminating the lower half of her face. The smile that lingered on her lips moments before had vanished.

He faced her, his heart hammering. The playful banter, her wide smile—didn't that add up to the possibility of something more meaningful? Admittedly, he was out of practice when it came to flirting, but she wasn't exactly discouraging him.

Her eyes, questioning, searched his face.

Letting go of her hair, he let his fingers brush against the sleeve of her denim jacket. He longed to cup her cheek with his palm and move in for a—

She cleared her throat and brushed past him. "It's almost midnight. We should go."

He dropped his chin to his chest. What was he thinking? Hadn't he spent the last few days trying to convince himself they couldn't be anything more than friends?

Chapter Six

On Sunday afternoon, Natalie stood at the front of a massive line, trying in vain to distract the children and their antsy parents waiting for a hay ride out to the pumpkin patch. She'd mentioned the absence of a line at the giant slide and passed out coupons for a free bag of kettle corn—anything to encourage families to visit another part of the farm before the pumpkin patch—but the crowd didn't budge. If she had any hope of sneaking away from the farm to check on the progress at the veteran's house, this line needed to shrink. People would start complaining, and she couldn't saddle Shelby with disgruntled customers.

Her phone vibrated in her back pocket. She reached for it, praying it was Rex letting her know he'd started a fourth tractor to tow yet another wagon for the hay ride.

A text from Mama illuminated the screen.

Please come by the house ASAP. Unexpected company.

Natalie shook her head and put her phone away. Not a chance. Mama would have to entertain her company on her own, which wouldn't be a problem. Southern hospitality was a gift she possessed plenty of.

"Here." She handed Shelby another handful of free drink coupons. "Desperate times call for desperate measures. If the wagons aren't back in time for the two o'clock run, start handing these out. Maybe if people can get a free bottle of water, they won't be quite so impatient."

"Yes, ma'am." Wide-eyed, Shelby took the coupons. "Where are you going?"

"I'm going to find Rex and see if he can fire up that fourth tractor. We need to get these people on their hay ride. It's too hot to stand out here very long."

"Please hurry."

"I will." She patted Shelby's arm. "You've got this. I'll be right back."

As she strode toward the golf cart parked nearby, her phone rang. Ignoring it, she broke into a jog, swiping her hand across her forehead at the moisture beading there. Last night's cool air had given way to another beautiful day, but the temperature had climbed over eighty degrees already. No wonder their customers were growing weary of standing in a long line. If Rex didn't bring that tractor around soon, they'd have to get creative. Fast.

Her phone was silent for an instant, and then it rang again. "Oh, brother." She paused and pulled her phone from her pocket. *Mama.* Jabbing at the screen, she answered the call while sliding behind the wheel. "Hello?"

"Well, it's about time. I've texted, called, called again—don't you answer your phone anymore?"

"Mama, the farm is swarming with people, we're short a tractor for the hay ride—"

"I'm happy to hear you're swamped. That's always a nice problem to have."

She silently counted to three. "What can I do for you, Mama?"

"Did you forget what day it is?"

She mentally scrolled through her packed calendar. "It's Sunday, isn't it?"

"Did you forget that your sister moves home from Alaska today?"

She winced. Kirsten had mentioned Tisha was on her way home. But she was stopping in Greensboro first, wasn't she? "I thought that was…tomorrow."

"Her new apartment in Greensboro isn't ready yet. Drop by. The two of you can sit on the porch and get reacquainted."

Reacquainted? If this was Mama's plan for resolving old conflicts, it didn't sound promising. "I—I don't think I can. Maybe if Rex gets the tractor running."

"Rex is more than qualified to handle things. That's why we hired him. You don't have to do everything yourself."

Natalie cringed at the subtle jab. That wasn't exactly true. If she didn't fix this, who would?

"I can't leave Shelby to deal with all of the customers and load the wagons alone."

"I'd like for you to come by." Mama's voice had taken on a frigid tone. "This is important. The hay rides are in capable hands."

Doubtful. She swallowed the terse response. Mama wouldn't appreciate being challenged.

"I'll see what I can do." Natalie ended the call without saying goodbye and dropped the phone on the cushion beside her. Tisha had spent the last five years in Alaska, bouncing between seasonal jobs. On the rare occasions, she had come home. Their relationship felt forced, as if it hadn't fully recovered from Tisha's horrible misstep that nearly ruined the farm. What Natalie truly wanted was someone she could trust to shoulder the burden of managing the farm—not someone who might jeopardize everything with a careless mistake. Forever Love had sent her a contract, and she had to admit that their offer was appealing. But if she accepted, how could she leave knowing there wasn't anyone to step up and keep the business running? Her thoughts circled back around to the benefits of a significant financial windfall. It would relieve the burden of funding Daddy's care, but that didn't make it any easier to tell her family.

She heaved a sigh and steered the golf cart toward the shed where Rex maintained all their equipment. Parking in front of the open doorway, she hopped out. Rex stood staring at the engine of their oldest red tractor, the leathery skin of his brow furrowed. "How's it going?"

He lifted his John Deere hat and scratched his almost bald head. "I don't know, Miss Natalie. I've about tried everything I can think of."

"It won't start?"

"Nope." He replaced his hat. "If it's all right with you, I'd like to consult your daddy. Think he's up to it?"

"I—I don't know. It's worth a try. He might welcome the distraction."

Rex grinned. "Your mama getting to him?"

Natalie chuckled. "No, I didn't say that. Mama mentioned my sister Tisha came home a day early."

"Oh. Well, maybe I shouldn't bother him."

"He might want a break from all the excitement. It wouldn't hurt to ask. Feel free to borrow the golf cart." Her smile faded. Daddy could probably still tinker with the tractor, but he couldn't handle the walk from the house to the shed.

"Thank you. I believe I'll take you up on that."

Rex sped off in the golf cart. Natalie realized too late that she'd left her phone lying on the seat. Oh, well. A few minutes without it might do her some good. She left the shed, cutting back across the grass toward the hay rides. As was often the case when she was alone, her thoughts turned to Shay—especially after last night. Butterflies flitted through her abdomen. The expression on his face as they walked in the moonlight, his hand lingering on her arm—she was certain he was going to kiss her. It took every ounce of self-control she possessed to walk away and get in her SUV. They'd kept conversation to a minimum on the short drive to his house. If he was offended, he hid it well. But now she couldn't stop wishing for another opportunity to be near him. Shaking her head, she kicked at a rock in her path. So not a good idea. No matter how often she repeated her mantra not to date another firefighter, that smile of his made her want to break her own rule.

All hope of a productive afternoon working side by side with Shay vanished when she saw the scene unfolding at the hay rides. The line had grown even longer, and a man towered over Shelby, his hands balled in fists and his face as red as a beet. *Oh, no.*

Natalie raced toward them, closing the distance quickly. She stopped next to Shelby, whose eyes brimmed with tears. "Excuse me, I'm the manager here. Is everything okay?"

"No, everything is not okay. This is ridiculous. We've been standing out here in the hot sun for over forty-five minutes. These kids want a pumpkin, and you people can't seem to get your act together."

She held up her hand. "I can assure you we're doing everything possible to add a fourth tractor and keep the line moving."

"Where?" He craned his neck. "I don't see no tractor."

"Right." She offered a tight smile. "We have three tractors working hard to carry our guests safely to and from the pumpkin patch. As soon as the fourth one is ready, we'll bring—"

"That's unacceptable." He swept his hand toward the crowd fanned out behind him. "These people deserve better."

"I'm sorry, sir. We're doing everything we can. Wagons leave on the half hour. If you'd prefer to see another part of the farm and come back later, we offer plenty of options."

"And lose my spot in line? No way." He linked his arms across his barrel chest and glared at her. "I'm not moving until I see a wagon. Then my son and I plan to get on it."

"Very well. Then I'm going to ask you to please lower your voice and stop yelling at my employees."

"Maybe if your employees did their job and didn't let tractors break, I wouldn't have to raise my voice, now, would I?"

Shelby's sharp intake of breath underscored Natalie's own shock. This guy was a piece of a work. The sound of an approaching tractor saved her from any further interaction. While Shelby went and helped unload the passengers and their pumpkins, Natalie gave them a few minutes to clear out and then unhooked the rope barrier. "Enjoy your hay ride," she murmured, stepping out of the way for the man and his son to claim their spot.

The next two tractors arrived in quick succession, and she loaded the wagons. Finally, the line dwindled to a manageable size, and the customers seemed happy to wait. Rex rolled up in the golf cart, Daddy riding shotgun, with a blonde in the back.

"Tisha?" The name died on Natalie's lips. It looked like Mama's preferences trumped hers. Again. Natalie would have to speak with her sister whether she wanted to or not.

Shay lingered at the building site until close to four o'clock Sunday afternoon, finding more things to work on and hoping Natalie showed up. Wasn't that the plan? Every time a car went by on the highway, he strained to see if it slowed and made the turn toward the cul-de-sac. Maybe he'd scared her off last night when he'd almost kissed her. She hadn't reacted well—hustling to her SUV, and then driving him home with little more than polite conversation.

He hammered one more nail into the drywall. So much for trying to be spontaneous. An alarm chimed on his phone, reminding him he needed to head home before the boys finished their naps. He liked to be there when they woke up, and he was cutting it close.

Outside, Hamilton and one of his buddies were loading their tools into the back of a truck. "We're calling it a day, too. Want to join us at The End Zone for a burger?"

"I can't." Shay tapped his watch. "I need to relieve the babysitter."

"Doesn't your mama watch your kids?"

"She does. If I want her to help me again anytime soon, I'd better give her a break."

An impish grin spread across Hamilton's face. "You know what they say about all work and no play."

Shay ignored the jab and strode toward his own truck. Whomever coined that phrase must not have been a single parent. "Catch you later," he called back over his shoulder as he climbed behind the wheel.

As he drove away, a hollow ache filled his chest. The boys were the best gifts God had given him. He couldn't imagine life without them. But he missed having a normal social life—grabbing a burger on a Sunday night, jawing about whatever game the restaurant played on the flat-screen TVs. The days when he could blow off his chores to watch a whole football game felt like a lifetime ago.

Shay slowed to a stop at the end of the street, his gaze wandering across the highway to the farm. A steady line of cars streamed into the entrance. Could he convince Mom to help him take the boys over to play? Fresh air and activity helped the evenings and bedtime routines go smoothly. Dad wasn't supposed to be home from his trip yet, so maybe she'd stick around for a few more hours. Finding a break in the traffic, he merged onto the highway and rehearsed what he might say to Natalie when he saw her again. Their next encounter was sure to be awkward, especially if he had his mother and kids tagging along.

When he pulled into his driveway, Mom came out onto the porch. She stood on the top step, pressing a finger to her lips.

He got out and eased his door closed. "Still asleep?"

She nodded. "Going on three hours."

"Awesome." He climbed the steps and planted a quick kiss on her cheek. "Thanks for taking care of them."

"Anytime. Now that you're home, I'm going to scoot."

"Oh?" He tried to mask his disappointment.

"Your father called. They caught plenty of fish, so they're headed home. If I'm about to have a freezer full, I need to make some space."

"Of course." Shay followed her inside the house. What she really meant was she wanted to get home before Dad did and perhaps not disclose where she'd spent the weekend. Dad would have something to say if he knew she'd "worked" on her days off.

After gathering her overnight bag and keys, she smiled up at him. "Thanks again for letting me stay with you. I fixed some soup. It's not much, but it will tide you over for a day or so. There's salad in the fridge, too."

"Mom," he whispered. "You didn't have to do that."

"I know. I wanted to." She patted his arm. "See you soon."

"Thanks again for your help." He closed the door behind her and secured the dead bolt.

Decision time. Taking the boys out alone planted an icy ball in the pit of his stomach. They didn't move fast, but there were still two of them, and he'd spend the entire time feeling tugged in opposite directions. While Aiden and Liam adored the farm, they had clear preferences on what to see and do first. With their limited vocabulary, Shay couldn't always figure out what Aiden wanted. If he wasn't careful, Liam would plow ahead, leaving Aiden in a heap of tears. Yet staying home meant refereeing at least half a dozen conflicts between supper and bedtime. It also meant not seeing Natalie.

"Daddy?"

"Da-da?"

Shay smiled at their sweet voices coming through the monitor on the kitchen counter. Making his way down the hall toward their bedroom, he heard more chatter that he couldn't quite decipher. He pushed open the door and found them both standing in one crib, wearing only their diapers and sleepy smiles.

"What are you monkeys up to?"

"Daddy, jump?" Liam gripped the railing and bounced up and down.

Aiden collapsed in the crib, laughter bubbling from his lips.

"Sure, I can jump." Shay mimicked Liam's movements, hopping up and down on the floor.

"No, no." Liam stopped, his little brow furrowed. "Jump there. Out there." He pointed at the window.

"Outside?"

"No, no. Farm. Farm."

Aiden climbed to his feet again, echoing his twin. "Arm. Arm."

"You want to go to the farm again? To the bounce house?"

"Yes, yes," Liam yelled, trying to climb over the rail.

"Whoa, easy there, tiger." Shay reached for him before he figured out how to vault over the side. That's all he needed—twin two-year-olds who could get out of bed on their own. While he changed their diapers and helped them put their clothes back on, Shay gave in to their repeated requests for a visit to the farm. He was tired of playing it safe.

Natalie leaned on the fence, watching the kids squeal with delight as they fed the baby goats at the petting zoo. Normally their contagious energy brought a smile to her face and made her forget the troubles of the day. But Kirsten stood on her left, and Tisha to her right, like bookends, hemming her in. They carried on as if they'd never been apart, talking over top of one another—falling back into an easy pattern of communication Natalie had never been able to achieve with Tisha. So she listened, mumbling the obligatory, "Oh, is that right," when Tisha shared an interesting factoid about Alaska or mentioned some detail about her new boyfriend, Chase.

On the other side of the goats' pen, she saw Aiden and Liam cruising along at a rate that looked dangerously close to approaching face-plants. Shay jogged up behind them, a gray backpack slung over one shoulder. He lunged, grasping each of the boys' hands in his own. Natalie stilled. He hadn't seen her yet, but it would only be a minute or so before he did. He knelt between the twins and spoke softly, the bill of his well-loved baseball cap pulled low on his brow. Was he worried about the boys touching the animals? Their conversation about his anxiety over taking them out alone replayed in her mind.

"Check out the cute dad with the twins." Kirsten nudged her in the side with her elbow. "Is he the new firefighter I've heard so much about?"

"Uh-huh." Who was talking about Shay and his kids? She didn't trust herself to ask. Tisha might've been away a long time, but she'd see right through

Natalie's pathetic attempts to conceal her attraction to Shay.

"Those little boys are adorable," Tisha murmured. "Are you going to go talk to him?"

Natalie shrugged. "Maybe." She should. Knowing he was stressed and not offering to help seemed heartless. But with her sisters for an audience...

Kirsten leaned uncomfortably close, her gaze zeroing in on Natalie's face. "Are you blushing?"

"Stop." Natalie backed away. "Of course not. I've been out in the sun all afternoon."

"Right." Kirsten bit back a smile and exchanged knowing looks with Tisha.

Shay chose that exact moment to stand up, his gaze meeting hers across the enclosure. A hesitant smile curved up one corner of his mouth. "Hey."

"Hi." Natalie managed an awkward wave.

"Mercy," Kirsten whispered. "If you're not going to talk to him, I will."

"Not on your life." Natalie pushed off from the railing and left Tisha and Kirsten to their junior high commentary. Even though she entertained thoughts of leaving Meadow Springs, there was no way she'd stand back and let her sister flirt with Shay. She stopped where Aiden and Liam stood, petting the goats.

"How's it going?" Shay asked, not relinquishing his grip on the boys' shoulders.

"I'm all right. How are y'all?"

Either Liam or Aiden—she was embarrassed to

admit she couldn't tell them apart—glanced up at her. A grin reminiscent of his father's spread across his little face, and he pivoted, arms outstretched.

Her heart fluttered. She glanced at Shay for approval. "Is it okay if I pick him up?"

"Of course. But he'll want you to carry him around for the rest of the night."

Would that be a bad thing? She leaned down and scooped the little boy up, resting him on her hip. Oh, she'd definitely hear about this later. She refused to look across the goat pen, focusing instead on the cutie snuggling against her.

He studied her face, his pudgy fingers flicking at one of her hoop earrings.

"What's happening, big guy? Do you like the goats?"

His mouth formed a perfect 'o' as he flicked her earring again.

"Aiden." Shay's firm tone caught the boy's attention. His head swiveled around.

"Be gentle with Miss Natalie, please."

"Or else I might have to tickle you." She walked her fingers across his tummy, eliciting a giggle as he tried to grab her hand.

Shifting Aiden to her other hip, she glanced at Shay. "Thanks for saying his name. I didn't want to ask…"

"I figured. Even my mom gets mixed up. Here's a hint—Aiden always wears something green."

She looked him over. Sure enough, he sported a

green T-shirt with characters she didn't recognize playing soccer. Wow. She had a lot to learn about hanging with the toddler crowd.

"What about Liam? Does he have an assigned color?"

"Depends. He's harder to reason with, although he prefers blue." Shay lifted one of Liam's arms in the air. "He also has a birthmark on his wrist that's easy to spot."

Birthmark. Wrist. Got it. She filed the information away for safe-keeping.

Shay swung his gaze in Kirsten and Tisha's direction. "Who are your friends?"

She smiled through clenched teeth. "Two of my sisters."

"Am I allowed to meet them?" His eyes twinkled.

"Allowed?" She tilted her head to one side, studying him. "That implies I'm keeping you from something."

"They haven't stopped staring at me since I got here, while you're pretending they don't exist."

Again with the flaming cheeks. Did she have to be so transparent? "Why don't we take the boys over to the inflatables? There's hardly anyone jumping right now."

"Sounds good to me." Shay tugged Liam's hand. "C'mon, buddy. Time to bounce."

Liam opened and closed his little fist in a backward wave. "Bye, goat."

"Bye," Aiden whispered, gripping Natalie's shoulder tighter.

They made their way over to the inflatable castle, Aiden narrating their walk with a steady stream of chatter. She couldn't understand anything he said.

Shay leaned close. "Don't worry, I have to ask Liam to interpret sometimes."

His fresh, clean scent, coupled with his deep voice, sent a delicious tingle zinging through her.

Aiden wiggled in her arms, drawing her back to reality. "Hang on. Let's sit here for a second." She lowered him to the wooden bench nearby and helped him peel off his sneakers and socks.

Shay led both boys to the entrance and boosted them inside. "There you go. Be careful."

Natalie fully expected he'd stay there, inches away from the mesh walls, ready to intervene in a second if the boys needed him. Much to her surprise, he turned and joined her on the bench, dropping his backpack at his feet.

"Do you and your sisters get along?"

She sighed. "It's complicated."

"Do these complications have anything to do with the farm?"

"Sort of." Natalie picked at a hangnail on her thumb. "Kirsten and I get along well. Tisha just moved back from Alaska. We have some unresolved issues, and I'm afraid things are going to get messy."

Shay slung his arm across the back of the bench.

"I'm guessing this is about more than borrowing clothes without asking or hogging the bathroom."

"She tried to lease our land to a solar energy company and—it's a long story, but it would've ruined us if we hadn't stopped her. Our land would've been tied up in a lease for years."

"Whoa." He grimaced. "I would've moved to Alaska, too."

"Mama asked her to come back when Daddy got sick."

"Do you wish she'd stayed?"

"I think it will be better for everyone if she lives in Greensboro, like she planned."

"But then she won't be around to help out."

"I'm not sure that would be a bad—"

One of the boys cried out, and Shay jumped off the bench without saying another word.

Way to go. Natalie jogged after him, scolding herself for going on and on about Tisha when they should've been paying attention to Aiden and Liam. As the crying escalated, she craned her neck to see what was the matter. If the boys were injured because she'd distracted Shay, she'd feel horrible. The last thing he needed was a toddler with a concussion, or worse, a broken bone.

Shay climbed inside the inflatable castle, his bare knees squeaking against the warm vinyl. Liam and Aiden lay in a heap in the middle, crying. Four other children stood around them, staring.

"It's okay, buddy. I'm here." He sank down beside them, gently pulling Liam into his arms. Liam clung to him, wailing. "Shhh, you're going to be all right."

Aiden crawled over and fell against Shay, tears tracking down his flushed cheeks. An angry bump had already formed on his forehead, the skin turning purple-blue.

His heart squeezed. They should've stayed home, after all.

"What happened?" Natalie stood outside the castle, one hand pressed against the mesh barrier, her eyes clouded with concern.

"I don't know." He tried not to sound curt. This wasn't her fault.

"Can I get you anything? An ice pack?"

Leaning back, he gently smoothed Liam's hair away from his forehead. Liam dipped his chin, his little body trembling. "Let me take a look." A goose egg similar to Aiden's marred the smooth skin above one eye.

Shay held him close and made a feeble attempt to sway side to side on the uneven surface. With his free hand, he rubbed Aiden's back.

"Shay?" Natalie prompted. "Do you want me to get some ice?"

"Please. They both need it."

"No problem. I'll be right back." Natalie turned and jogged away. The other children had scampered off, leaving the three of them alone. Aiden and Liam's cries had decreased to pathetic whimpers. Situations like this made him wish more than ever that he wasn't doing this parenting thing alone. Monica had gone off to chase her dreams, leaving him flailing to keep his head above water.

Why? Why did you leave? A lump clogged his throat. He tried not to think of her too often, much less allow self-pity to gain any traction. But he couldn't forget the bond he'd forged with Monica from slogging through the new-parent trenches. Together. At least, he'd thought they were a team. She'd obviously had other plans percolating all along.

"Da-da?" Aiden wriggled closer, making Liam squeal in protest as they fought over the much-coveted space on Shay's lap.

"Boys." He shifted and sat cross-legged, nestling one boy on each of his thighs. "Relax, I can hold both of you."

Aiden jammed his thumb in his mouth, while Liam pooched out his lower lip. "Hungry."

Shay's stomach rumbled, echoing Liam's simple declaration. "Me, too. We'll eat soon."

Supper sat in the cooler in the back of the truck. His valiant attempt to take the boys out for the evening and feed them seemed foolish now. As soon as Natalie brought the ice, and he felt certain the boys were okay, he'd head home.

"Here you go," she called from behind him.

He looked over his shoulder. Natalie popped her

head through the opening and held up two small Ziploc baggies.

"Thank you. I'll, um…" None of his EMT training had prepared him for convincing his own two-year-olds to put ice on their foreheads.

"I have a secret weapon, but I wanted to ask your permission first." Natalie kept one hand behind her back.

"What is it?" He set Liam on his feet first, and then prodded Aiden to stand, too. "Let's go, boys. We're done here."

"No, no." Liam shook his head.

"Maybe I should spell it," Natalie said.

"Okay." Shay crawled to the entrance on hands and knees. "Boys, c'mon. We're done."

"P-o-p-s-i-c-l-e-s?" Natalie scooted out of the way, giving him room to climb out of the inflatable.

He hesitated.

"If you're concerned it will ruin their supper, I won't be offended if you say no." She turned so the boys couldn't see them and showed him the cardboard box. "They're pretty healthy. I mean, as healthy as a Popsicle can be, right? I bought them for a summer camp we did in August. I even have two of the same flavor."

Shay softened at her hopeful smile. She was handling this whole scenario better than he was. "Let's try the ice bags first, all right?"

"Um, sure." She darted toward the bench and concealed the treats behind his backpack.

Shay helped Aiden to the ground first.

"Aiden, come sit with me." Natalie patted her lap with her hands.

The little boy toddled over, his recent collision apparently forgotten.

Liam eyed them both from the castle's opening, his pale eyebrows knitted together.

"We need to put ice on your forehead." Shay stretched out his arms.

Liam scowled and stepped out of reach.

"Son." He offered a stern warning and moved closer.

Liam retreated farther.

Shay sighed and dropped his chin to his chest. Was he really going to have to resort to bribery?

"If you'll put the ice on your head, I'll give you a Popsicle."

Liam's eyes widened. "'Sickle?"

"It's kind of like ice cream. On a stick."

That's all it took. Liam flipped onto his belly and, refusing Shay's help, lowered himself to the ground. He then raced to Natalie as fast as his little legs could carry him.

Shay followed, shaking his head. "I can't believe I'm negotiating with a toddler."

Natalie smiled up at him, Aiden balanced on her lap with the ice bag pressed against his forehead.

His chest tightened. As Aiden leaned into her embrace, twisting a section of her long hair around his little hand, Shay realized he'd never been jealous of his own son until that moment.

Aiden nestled his head against Natalie's shoulder and released a contented sigh. The plastic bag drooped in her hand, more water than ice. It seemed silly to keep holding it against his forehead, but he'd started this adorable little gesture of twirling her hair around his hand a while ago. She hated to move and ruin the tender moment. It seemed he wasn't the only Campbell man who had a thing for her hair.

She bit her lip to keep from smiling and stole a quick glance at Shay. He wasn't amused. Despite his repeated promises that Liam would get a Popsicle if he cooperated, a battle of wills played out between them. A muscle in Shay's cheek twitched again. He'd probably blow his stack any second.

Shifting her weight, she removed the bag and tried to examine Aiden's forehead. He turned away, popping his thumb in his mouth. *What a cutie.* Natalie resisted the urge to plant a quick kiss on his hair. She could stay like this for another hour, but the long shadows spilling across the ground reminded her she couldn't linger much longer. Being late for supper on Tisha's first night home was out of the question.

She cleared her throat. "I hate to go, but Mama and Daddy are expecting me for supper."

Shay tossed his own ice bag on the ground and sagged against the bench. Liam stared up at him, eyes questioning. "I'll distract them while you sneak away."

Poor guy. He looked wiped out. He'd flipped his baseball cap around backward, revealing the dark shadows under his eyes.

Should she invite them to supper? The idea was almost laughable. Mama would welcome them but read her the riot act later. Yet leaving him here to fend for himself seemed cruel. "W-would you like to come? There's plenty of food."

Shay stilled, his hand inside the Popsicle box. "That's sweet of you to invite us, but we can't crash your party. Especially not tonight."

"They'd love to meet you." For the second time in a matter of minutes, she wanted to snatch her words back the second they left her lips.

He tilted his head, studying her. "If you thought I was anxious and overprotective before, you should see me trying to feed my kids in front of strangers. Talk about a disaster waiting to happen."

Of course. The food allergy thing. Why didn't she remember that? "Maybe some other time." She looked down at Aiden, who showed little interest in the sweet treats Shay had revealed. Short of forcing him off her lap, she wasn't sure how to convince him to move.

"C'mon, Aiden. Miss Natalie has to go home." Shay motioned for him to come closer.

Aiden's hand slowed, only to resume twirling again.

"Aiden." Shay frowned. "Come here, please."

"Would it be easier if I helped you take them to your truck? Then we'd—"

"No."

She recoiled at his terse response.

"Go. We'll be fine."

"I'll see you later, Aiden." She maneuvered him onto the bench beside her, and then she quickly stood and backed away.

Aiden's face crumpled, and he tried to get down.

Shay splayed his hand across Aiden's chest. "No. Stay."

Natalie shot him a pleading look.

He shook his head, his expression masked. "Please. Just go."

"See you around." Natalie walked away, Aiden's cries trailing after her. Picking up the pace, she ducked her head and weaved through a crowd of people strolling along the path, praying none of her employees saw her.

Had she misread Shay's signals? If he didn't want her getting involved in his life or spending time with his kids, why did he keep coming around? Why didn't he stay home or take the boys to the park, instead of showing up at the farm again?

She broke into a jog, desperate for the solace of

her own space. It didn't matter. This was probably all for her own good, anyway—God's way of protecting her from getting her hopes up about something that wasn't meant to be.

Chapter Seven

The setting sun bathed Mama and Daddy's screen porch in a pale orange glow. Natalie claimed her favorite wicker chair in the corner and tucked her legs underneath her. "Thank you for supper. That was delicious."

Mama smiled and passed her a mug of decaf coffee. "My pleasure, hon."

"So." Kirsten sat in a chair, in the opposite corner, cradling her own cup of coffee. "How were things at the bouncy castle this afternoon?"

While Mama had her back turned, Natalie shot her sister a warning glance. *Don't start.*

Kirsten grinned and took a sip of her coffee.

Mama sank onto the wicker sofa next to Tisha, balancing a china teacup and saucer on her lap.

"Is Daddy going to join us?" Natalie asked, catching a glimpse of Daddy through the window, his lips pursed in concentration as he moved deliberately in their direction. He'd hardly said a word during supper.

"He'll be out in a few minutes." Mama sipped her tea, one dainty pinky in the air. "This will be a nice time for us to catch up."

"Isn't there football on TV tonight? He never misses a game." Daddy definitely wouldn't choose "girl talk" over watching sports. "Has he heard any news from the doctor yet?"

Mama's expression tightened, and then she recovered with a wobbly smile. "He'll be out here shortly."

Natalie's stomach twisted. "Mama—"

"Tell us more about this new man of yours." Mama patted Tisha's knee. "Have you met his family?"

Here we go. Hadn't they covered this already? Conversation over supper had focused on little else. Mama beamed like a pageant queen—one of her daughters had a boyfriend. Be still my heart.

"Chase has a wonderful family." Tisha's glowing expression rivaled Mama's. "We met his parents for dinner in Anchorage…"

While they dished about Chase's life in Alaska, Natalie's thoughts turned to Shay and his boys. Had Aiden recovered from his meltdown? Her heart ached. Poor thing.

"Natalie?" Kirsten called her name. "Are you still with us?"

"Sorry. You caught me daydreaming."

"Is he tall? Wears a baseball hat?" Kirsten wiggled her eyebrows.

"Has two little boys?" Tisha added.

Mama's gaze flitted across the porch, landing on Natalie. "Anything you'd like to share?"

"No."

"Oh, please." Kirsten rolled her eyes. "I saw the way he smiled at you. Don't even try to tell me you're just friends."

"Fine." Natalie lifted one shoulder. "I wasn't planning on telling you a thing."

"Does he really have small children?" Mama frowned.

Natalie dug her fingernails into her palm. "Yes, he does. Twin boys."

"Oh, sweetheart. Falling for a man who's already been...around the block is asking for trouble."

Around the block? Natalie glared daggers across the porch. "Please don't assume you know the truth about a man you haven't even met."

An awkward silence hung heavy in the growing twilight.

"Well." Mama cleared her throat. "I'm happy at least one of my daughters has found a nice man. Your father and I were beginning to wonder if we're ever going to have a wedding in this family."

Wow. That was uncalled for. It wasn't like she and Spencer hadn't made long-term plans. She'd suspected he'd intended to propose. Natalie stifled a sharp retort. Maybe this was the clarity she needed.

Forever Love's offer meant a fresh start in Charlotte, where the reminders of Spencer didn't—

Daddy's slow, shuffling steps onto the porch and the tears brimming in his eyes captured her attention. "Oh, no."

Silence blanketed the porch as Daddy's gaze met Mama's. Tisha and Kirsten exchanged worried glances.

"It's bad, isn't it?" Natalie whispered.

Daddy nodded, his lower lip trembling. "I'm afraid so. Doctor Armistead called on Friday. I've been waiting for the right time to tell you, but I guess there's never a right time—the test results confirmed what he already suspected. I have Lou Gehrig's."

Kirsten gasped, and Tisha pressed her fingers to her lips while her eyes welled.

No. Natalie dropped her chin to her chest, squeezing her eyes shut against the hot sting of tears.

Confident the boys were asleep, Shay padded into the living room and grabbed the remote control. Maybe he could finally relax and watch a movie. Mindless distraction was exactly what he needed. He sank into his leather couch and surfed the channels until he recognized the opening scenes of *Rudy.* Perfect. One of his favorites.

So why did he have a tough time paying attention? It wasn't the pile of unfolded laundry filling the love seat that captured his thoughts, either. Natalie's blue eyes on his, her tenderness as she comforted Aiden—all of it proved much more interesting than watching a bunch of guys chase a football. Twenty minutes later, he gave up and clicked off the TV. Tiptoeing into the kitchen, he opened a cabinet silently and grabbed a plastic water bottle. If a movie wouldn't quiet his thoughts, he'd try exercise. He filled the container with water from the dispenser on the refrigerator door and then twisted the cap on. Halfway to the garage door, he went back and grabbed the portable video monitor from the counter.

Out in the garage, he stood in the middle of the crowded space, surveying the neat stack of moving boxes still lining the far wall. Did those things multiply? For every box he'd emptied, it seemed two more appeared in its place. He'd revisit that daunting task another day. Right now he needed to burn off some steam. He placed the monitor on the empty workbench. The screen projected a black-and-white image of the boys snuggled in one crib, reassuring him he could work out in peace.

What a night. After he'd wrangled the boys into the truck and brought them home from the farm, they'd stalled at the table—dragging supper out until he couldn't stand another minute of their whining. Then he'd slogged his way through the mundane routine of books, bath and bedtime. It had taken an extra reading of Aiden's favorite story to get him to quit babbling about Natalie.

He squeezed his eyes shut. Natalie's stricken expression reappeared. Man, he'd hated turning down her offer for supper. But his stupid insecurities trumped all else, and he let her—no, asked her to—go, leaving him with a brokenhearted Aiden. Shay opened his eyes, determined to push past his disappointment over how the evening had ended. He strode across the cement floor to the stationary bike parked in the corner.

We're destined to fail...aren't we?

The thought had meandered through his mind all evening. Longer than that, really. Ever since he'd used the lead about the electrician as an excuse to stop by the barn the other night, he'd entertained the possibility of there being a "we." Tonight he'd made a big show of being the logical one and reminding Natalie that her family didn't need company. He wasn't truly motivated by manners and common sense. Not at all.

She was charming and easygoing—not to mention beautiful. Her ability to work hard and do the right thing for another family in the community—even when it seemed an uphill climb—only made him admire her more. She'd done everything right—respected his boundaries, offered assistance when the boys were injured... But catching a glimpse of her as a permanent part of his future scared him.

He slid the water bottle into the holder on the bike's frame and settled onto the uncomfortable seat. Grasping the smooth handles, he punched the buttons on the screen, choosing a rather unforgiving routine with plenty of steep hills. As he pedaled, he reminded his traitorous heart of all the reasons why he and his fragile little family couldn't afford to fall for Natalie. There was too much at stake. As he ramped up the speed, his lungs and muscles burning, the reality of his conflicted emotions weighed on him. He had a sneaking suspicion it was too late. He'd already fallen for her. Hard.

Fortified with a second cup of coffee to combat the ache throbbing in her head, Natalie sat at her desk in her office early Monday morning and stared at her computer screen. Staying focused was a challenge. The tumultuous emotions twisting her insides in knots had kept her awake, punching her pillow into the wee hours. With a heavy sigh, she pushed back her chair and stood. She'd finish payroll and place an order for The Grille later. Now she needed a project—a welcome distraction from the upcoming phone call with Forever Love on Thursday, the devastating news about Daddy and a certain handsome firefighter.

Dew still clung to the grass as she approached the highway. Natalie shivered, waiting as a school bus rolled by, leaving a pungent trail of diesel fumes in its wake. A break in the traffic offered an opportunity to jog across to the other side.

No way. A roof? When did that happen?

Trent had texted her a picture of the A-shaped trusses going up on Friday, but she never imagined they'd make so much progress in one weekend. Two men wearing harnesses over their jeans and T-shirts were anchored to the peak, their nail guns firing in quick succession as they put down shingles.

"Good morning." She stopped in the driveway, cupping her hand over her eyes to shield against the sunshine.

Hamilton peered over the edge of the roof. "Mornin'. We're getting an early start. I hope you don't mind."

"Mind? Are you kidding? I'm thrilled. Thank you for being here."

"You're welcome."

She climbed the steps, stopping in the entryway. Her hopeful optimism waned. Not much had changed in the kitchen or living area. Somehow they had to figure out a way to get cabinets donated. The chance that someone would do a custom build for an entire kitchen in less than a month was, well, almost impossible. She flinched as the nail guns fired off another round. The roof, though... how awesome was that?

Her sneakers made a clomping sound across the plywood floors as she strode down the hall. At least the drywall was coming along. Maybe her plan for painting the smallest bedroom today wasn't such a far-fetched idea, after all. She peeked into the first room—the one where Shay had helped with the floor. Despite her best efforts to banish him from her thoughts, just standing here reminded—

"Natalie?"

Wait. What? Clearly she needed more coffee if she imagined Shay calling her name.

"Natalie, are you here?" Footsteps moved closer. She leaned around the door frame.

Shay stood in the middle of the living room, hands jammed in the back pockets of those faded jeans he wore so well. His tentative smile and clean-shaven skin made her knees quake.

"Hey." She forced herself to maintain eye contact. "What are you doing here?"

"I took the boys over to Trent and Caroline's house. She offered to take them to story time at the library. He mentioned the guys were working on the roof, so I thought I'd stop by."

"How are the—"

"Are you…." He trailed off. "Excuse me. Ladies first."

"How are the boys?" She touched her fingertips to her brow. "Their heads?"

"They're fine. Back to their usual tricks this morning."

"Good. I'm glad."

"Thanks for your help yesterday. I don't know what I would've done if you hadn't been there."

"That's nice of you to say. I'm afraid I wasn't all that helpful." Poor Aiden. She bit her lower lip. They'd all be better off if she'd steered clear of the Campbell men.

Shay's eyebrows arched toward his still-damp hair. "Are you kidding? I can barely handle it when one cries, let alone both. Seriously. You were a huge help."

"If you say so."

"What are you working on? Plumbing? Ceiling fan installation?" His tone defused the tension creeping into the conversation.

"Very funny. The family our committee selected to receive the house is expecting their second child around Thanksgiving. I'd love to get started on the nursery."

"Let's have a look. Maybe there's something we can do." He joined her in the doorway of the small bedroom. Her skin tingled at his nearness. She eased farther into the room, careful not to let his arm brush against hers.

"The electrician's been here already." Shay pointed to the exposed wires dangling from the middle of the ceiling. "That's good news."

"No windows yet, though." Natalie frowned at the thick plastic hanging over the opening along the far wall.

"Easy there, negative Nancy. I'm trying to look on the bright side." Despite the intentional space she'd created, Shay filled it with a playful nudge of his elbow.

"You're right. I should be more grateful for all the hard work that's gone into this project. I'm still worried we're not going to finish in time."

"Let's do something about that." He bent over and lifted a white carton from the floor. "How do you feel about spackle?"

She chuckled. "No one's ever asked me that before."

"There's a first time for everything, right?" He offered her a plastic putty knife. "It's not quite the same as painting, but it's still an important step."

She took the knife and waited while he popped open the lid. "Are you going up on the roof?"

"Me? Not today. I think they've got the manpower they need up there. I'd rather stay in here and help you."

"Oh. Right." She ducked her head, flustered by his nearness and the scent of his soap or aftershave teasing her senses. Did his ex-wife realize all that she'd given up? What kind of woman left two adorable little boys, not to mention their handsome father?

She needed to rein in her thoughts. Carving the edge of the knife through the white mud, she smeared it over a nail head on the wall. It wasn't any of her business.

"I probably have another knife in my truck. I'll be right back."

She worked in silence, repeating the process of scoop, smear and flatten. There was something therapeutic about the task—filling in the pockmarks with a dollop of goop and then smoothing out the lumps. If only she could resolve all her issues with such a simple solution.

"How about some music?" Shay returned with a toolbox and a portable stereo that had seen better days. "This was sitting in the front room. Do you think anyone would mind if we borrowed it?"

She glanced at the gray plastic coated with dust and spatters of dry paint. "Wow. I haven't seen a boom box like that in years."

"As long as we have electricity, let's see what we can come up with." He plugged it in, pressed the power button and then twisted the dial until the static gave way to Jayce Philips's latest hit song. Natalie hummed along with the familiar lyrics while she worked. "I love Jayce's new album. I hope he performs this song when he comes. Have you heard it?"

Shay glanced at the speaker and frowned. "No, I don't think so. I'm not much of a country fan."

"Really. I would've totally pegged you as an old-school country music guy. A little Merle Haggard… maybe some George Strait or Alan Jackson."

His disbelieving stare confirmed she couldn't have been more wrong. "All right, I'm stumped. Name your top three favorite bands."

"Coldplay, Bon Jovi, Hootie & the Blowfish. Some classic rock is pretty good."

"Oh, Coldplay. They put on a good show." She smiled at the memory. "I still can't believe my parents let me go. Who was your first concert?"

"I begged my grandparents for tickets to Hootie & the Blowfish. They bought them. It was epic." He held up another putty knife. "Mind if I join you? I'd tackle a different wall, but I didn't see another container."

"Not a problem. I can share." She smiled and then brushed a strand of hair from her face. Shay didn't move. His eyes, two pools of emeralds, darkened as his gaze held hers. *Mercy*. Her pulse skittered out of control.

"What?" The word came out in a nervous laugh. "Do I have it in my hair?"

"No. Here." The pad of his thumb trailed across her cheekbone.

She stilled, her breath caught in her throat. His palm cupped her jaw, the warmth of his touch putting all her senses on high alert.

He lowered his head, brushing his lips against hers. Despite her intentions to keep all firefighters in the friends' zone, Natalie leaned into him. His lips were soft, and he tasted like mint. As Shay deepened the kiss, all logical thought slipped away, and she let the putty knife clatter to the floor. Her fingers skimmed up his arms, the soft fabric of his T-shirt a sharp contrast to the taut muscles rippling underneath.

"Natalie," he whispered, his voice ragged as he rested his forehead against hers.

She didn't want to open her eyes, didn't want the moment to end. Because pulling away meant facing reality. Before Thursday afternoon, she had to choose between her dream job in a town four hours from home or staying in Meadow Springs. Four hours might as well be four states when it came to Shay. The kiss shouldn't have happened.

Natalie slipped from his grasp, her fingers pressed to her lips. A storm cloud of emotions rolled across her face.

Shay's gut clenched.

She dropped her hand and backed away. "I'm— We should..."

"I know, I know, focus on the task at hand. Got it."

"No." She shook her head. "I have to go."

"Funny thing, it doesn't do much for my confidence when you run after I kiss you." His lousy attempt at humor crashed and burned, as if the last five minutes never happened. She hadn't discouraged him. Until now. Her mouth moving against his... Her hands gripping his arms... Nothing about her response to his touch said "Stop." So why the hasty exit?

"I have to meet a client."

He followed her out into the hallway. "You have clients at nine thirty on a Monday?"

Natalie's spine went ramrod straight. She turned, her gaze challenging his. "I always meet Saturday's bride-to-be at the barn to go over any last-minute changes. I'd rather not meet her looking like this." She gestured to her worn Meadow Springs Crusaders T-shirt and paint-splattered jeans.

"Of course." He worked his jaw back and forth. "Tell Trent and Caroline I said 'Hey.'"

"Can I give you a ride over to the barn?"

She offered a wobbly smile. "No, thanks."

Wait. "Don't go."

Her smile faded. "Shay—"

"Please. Give me two minutes." He kneaded the back of his neck. "What happened?"

"That kiss… Aiden crying at the farm… My dad's health and the farm's future…" She pressed her palms to her flushed cheeks. "I'm a hot mess."

"I don't understand."

Dropping her hands to her sides, she paced the living area in a tight circle. "I just— Spencer's death was so hard. I thought I'd never be able to move on. Then I met you, and I—I started to think maybe… But you have two kids, and you're a firefighter. I'm juggling two businesses, plus my dad was just diagnosed with a horrible illness. The timing—it's crazy."

"Crazy good or crazy…impossible?"

Silence filled the space between them.

"You just told me everything I needed to know."

Natalie's lower lip trembled. "Please let me—"

"I don't want to keep you from your appointment. See you around." Without a backward glance, he strode down the hallway.

The local traffic report came through the speakers and echoed off the walls of the empty room. Shay retrieved his tool and glopped more spackle on nail heads, but it wasn't the same without Natalie beside him. Her comments churned in his head. Was his timing really that lousy? The chemistry between them was unmistakable. There's no way he'd read that wrong. Her hesitancy about dating another firefighter kind of made sense, although Spencer's death in an unfortunate accident didn't mean he'd suffer the same outcome. What did Aiden's meltdown have to do with anything? He was only two. Tantrums came with the territory. He scowled. Maybe she hadn't spent much time around little kids. Birthday parties and hay rides at the farm didn't exactly give her the whole picture.

The DJ on the radio segued from a commercial break, his exuberant tone jumping on Shay's last nerve. "Next up, the debut single from one of country music's rising stars. You'll be hearing a lot more from her in the near future. Her first album drops October twelfth. Here's Monica Ramsey with 'You Don't Know Me.'"

Shay pounced on the portable stereo and jabbed at the power button. The radio turned off before the opening chords of the song even began to play. His chest heaved as he glared at the speakers. There was no way he could listen to her sing. *Ramsey.* Her maiden name. What was up with that? Never in a million years did he expect she'd land a record deal.

Icy tentacles slithered around his heart. *Not fair.* She got an express ticket to fame, and he got... what? Lonely nights and the daunting task of raising their boys alone. *Thanks a lot, Monica.* Wonder what all her new fans would think if they knew the truth—she'd abandoned her family at the expense of her dreams. Who *did* that?

"I'm a hot mess..." Natalie's words echoed in his mind. He scrubbed his hand over his face. Sure, she had a lot going on, but isn't that what relationships were about? Walking together through the ups and downs of life? Did she honestly not want to make space in her life for a husband and children, or was she afraid?

So many questions. Maybe this wasn't the right time for a relationship. He wasn't in the best place emotionally, either. Disappointment twisted his gut as he scraped his knife clean and replaced the lid on the container. Better to recognize that now before either he or Natalie got hurt. They could remain friends, and he'd honor his commitment to this project. After it was finished, he'd keep a safe distance.

Still, the mental picture of Natalie shouldering her burdens alone deepened the hollow ache in his chest. Gathering up his toolbox, he headed out to his truck.

Natalie sat alone at an empty table in the middle of Magnolia Lane, peeling the label off a bottle of water. Thankfully she'd made it through the meeting without any major gaffes. Making the final arrangements before the big event was a familiar process, one she could repeat in her sleep. Yet the notes she'd collected on her iPad might as well be in a foreign language. Half-finished sentences and odd phrases filled the screen. Good thing Mrs. Sterling and the bride, Claire, were super organized. Otherwise Saturday's reception might be total chaos. She glanced at her checklist one more time. Did she finalize the headcount with the caterer? Or did Claire say she'd handle that?

While they'd peppered her with questions about last-minute details, all she could think about was Shay. His touch was…unnerving. That kiss had been unlike any she'd experienced in a very long time. Okay, maybe ever. No wonder she'd come undone, babbling about Aiden and timing and—

"Stupid, stupid girl." She groaned and tipped her head back, staring at the ceiling.

She'd crushed him with her thoughtless words. He'd tried to turn away before she saw the hurt in his eyes, but the pain was etched all over his face. No wonder he'd dismissed her before she could explain. That moment of silence had ruined everything. If only she could rewind and not...overthink everything. A weak laugh slipped from her lips. Like that was possible.

"Do you always talk to yourself?"

"Ack!" Natalie shot out of her chair, knocking it over onto the hardwood. She clutched her chest, her heart thundering against her ribs.

Tisha moved closer, her platinum blonde hair in a sleek ponytail and an amused expression on her face. She looked fantastic in skinny jeans, tall boots and a red sweater.

Natalie righted her chair. "You scared me to death."

"Sorry." Tisha sat down across the table, her eyes flitting to the iPad. "You took off last night, and we didn't get a chance to talk very much. What are you working on?"

"I didn't have time to hang out." She slid the tablet closer, ignoring the inquiry. "Some of us have responsibilities, you know."

Tisha arched an eyebrow. "Are you implying that I don't?"

She smoothed her clammy palms over her skirt and reclaimed her seat. "I thought you were in town for a quick visit."

"That's what I wanted to talk to you about." Tisha shifted in her chair. "Now that I'm home, I have a better understanding of what's going on. It's obvious Daddy's health isn't going to improve—"

"We don't know that. I've done some research. Some people live as long as twenty years after their diagnosis."

"Mama says it's most likely three to five."

Natalie cringed. She couldn't argue with that. Everything she'd read about the symptoms, combined with the doctor's feedback and the initial neurology consult, pointed toward a quick progression of the dreadful disease.

"Kirsten and I talked last night. I don't have to move to Greensboro. Chase is going to be busy flying, anyway."

Oh, no. Natalie balled her hands into fists, her nails digging into her palms. *Don't say it.*

Tisha reached over and pressed her fingers to Natalie's arm. "I'm here to help."

"Define *help*?" Natalie quoted the air with her fingertips. "Because, if memory serves me correctly—"

Tisha narrowed her gaze. "It's been five years. Don't you think it's time to let it go?"

Natalie looked down, rubbing her finger over a blemish on the table. Tisha was right about one thing—they didn't need to rehash the past. But she wasn't about to hand over the farm, either. "A lot has changed since you moved away. It's not like when we were kids. This is a huge operation."

"Then show me what's new. It can't be that much different. Let me manage half of the workload."

Natalie studied her sister's earnest expression.

"What happens when you decide a long-distance relationship doesn't work? What if Chase gets a promotion and you decide to move away?"

"We'll worry about that when it happens."

"It sounds to me like it could happen soon."

Tisha's gaze narrowed. "You don't always have to be the savior, you know."

"Excuse me?"

"The farm would survive without you. I know you find that hard to believe."

"I never said it wouldn't survive."

"Then why won't you let somebody else take over? Sometimes you have to trust that God will provide, even if His provision doesn't look like you think it should."

Natalie felt a muscle in her jaw twitch. "Maybe you missed the memo. He hasn't provided anyone else."

"Because nobody meets your ridiculous expectations." Tisha's voice raised an octave. "Your identity is all wrapped up in the farm and keeping all the plates spinning. Nobody else can do it because you won't let them."

Natalie pressed her lips into a thin line. "Wow. Don't hold back."

"I didn't come in here to hurt you."

"Really? You've got a funny way of showing it."

"Don't." Tisha's eyes brimmed with tears.

"Don't what?"

"Push me away. I'm not the same girl who ran

off to Alaska. Give me a chance. We have to pull together if our family's going to survive this."

"Guess what? While you've been gallivanting around the last frontier, I've been here, pulling with all I've got." She stood, her hands trembling as she tucked her things into her tote bag.

"Natalie, wait."

Spots peppered her vision. "Thanks for this chat. Your little pep talk was super helpful." She whirled away, her ballet flats skimming the hardwood floor as she crossed to the side door. Better to leave now before she said anything she'd regret later. Tisha had a lot of nerve calling her expectations ridiculous. Hadn't her tireless efforts and determination to strive for excellence kept the farm thriving, while Tisha had gone off and done exactly what she wanted?

Outside the barn, she squinted at the bright late-morning sunshine, hurt and confusion twisting her insides into knots. Laughter and shouts of delight filtered through the crisp air. They had three school groups visiting the farm today. *Please, please don't let me run into anyone right now.*

Head down, she chose the quickest route toward home, her conversation with her sister replaying in her mind. Tisha's words stung. Probably because there was an element of truth to them. She did hate the idea of relinquishing control of the farm to someone else. Especially to Tisha, whom she didn't trust to do a good job. If she was brutally honest, she had put a lot of faith in her own abilities, because God certainly hadn't cooperated with her plans when He'd allowed Spencer's death. So she'd stopped trusting Him.

Fatigue slowed her steps as she trudged toward her front door. Maybe this offer from Forever Love was part of God's plan for her future. Was He easing her out of her comfort zone and away from the very things that fueled her self-reliance?

Chapter Eight

The ambulance's flashing lights cast an eerie blue glow over the lawn. Shay's eyes felt like someone had poured ash in them. He yanked off his gloves and dragged his hand across his sweaty face. Trent stood nearby, spraying the charred remains of the two-story house with the fire hose. They didn't get many fire calls at 3:00 a.m. in Meadow Springs, but sadly, tonight they had. This one was a tough loss. All he wanted was a hot shower and a few hours of sleep.

Chief Murphy crossed the soggy grass and stopped in front of Shay, his gray eyes filled with empathy. Clapping Shay's back with his thick hand, he leaned close, raising his voice above the roar of the truck's engine. "You did the best you could."

He shook his head. "It wasn't enough."

"Some calls are like that."

"I thought for sure we could save the house, too." He swung his gaze toward the homeowners, a young family of five, huddled in a neighbor's front yard. The children hid their faces, but their trembling bodies made Shay's own heart ache. He and his partner had gone back in to perform a secondary search when the homeowners said their middle child—a six-year-old boy—was still inside. They'd found him hiding in his bedroom closet, and Shay had carried him to safety.

"The family is safe and accounted for. I know it sounds trite, but houses can be rebuilt. There's only one you."

Shay moistened his dry lips. Chief Murphy was right. That had been a close call. He'd battled dozens of house fires in his career. Tonight was the first time in years he'd feared not making it out. Thankfully they'd escaped the blazing inferno before the roof collapsed. His blood ran cold at the thought of what might've happened if they hadn't been able to find the boy.

"C'mon. Let's finish up and get back to the station."

"Yes, sir." Shay forced himself to move, his wobbly legs threatening to give way.

"Shay?" Chief Murphy called after him.

He glanced over his shoulder.

"I'm proud of you, son. Good job."

Not trusting himself to speak, Shay managed a quick nod before he turned away. It wasn't the casual use of the word *son* that got to him. As a veteran firefighter, and the one in charge, the chief sprinkled it throughout his conversations, both in serious and lighthearted moments. Maybe it was the outcome of tonight's fire, or the stark realization of the brevity of life, that clogged his throat with emotion. Or maybe it was the painful truth that his own father rarely—if ever—addressed him as "son," never mind paired it with praise.

While they stowed the ladders and retracted the hose, Shay kept his head down and worked quickly to complete his assigned tasks. On the chief's signal, he took his seat inside the engine behind Hamilton, their driver for this shift. As they pulled away from the scene, he turned from the window so he wouldn't have to see the ugly destruction left behind by the fire.

The ride back to the fire station lacked the usual banter, which was fine with him. Except for the dispatcher's voice on the radio, directing other emergency personnel, the cab remained quiet.

Once Hamilton parked the engine in the garage, Shay wasted little time getting out of his gear, praying he wouldn't have to put it all back on until his next shift. He raked his fingers through his matted hair, the acrid scent of smoke lingering as he hung up his jacket and pants next to Trent's.

"You did well tonight, Campbell." Trent secured his helmet on the wall hook.

"Thanks." Too tired to say more, he filed into the station behind the rest of the guys. They meant well, but these platitudes of encouragement that the chief and Trent offered didn't help. At all. Experiences like this dredged up all his past shortcomings—even the ones he never allowed himself to think about. Like the chief said, all the family members were accounted for. In the grand scheme of things, it could've been worse. But how could he tell Trent or the chief or anyone else that it wasn't that simple?

After a quick, hot shower he pulled on clean clothes and fell into his bunk. Less than two hours until his alarm rang. Hopefully they wouldn't have another call and he could rest his weary mind and body. As the new guy, he was supposed to get up first and have the coffee started and table set for breakfast.

Although he expected to be asleep before his head hit the pillow, his anxious thoughts tormented him. If he'd been gravely injured in the fire, what kind of life would the boys have? The dangerous nature of his work wasn't something he usually dwelled on. But that was his first brush with death since he had gained full custody. Dozens of calls at his old station in Virginia were more intense than a house fire. But he'd been younger. Naive. Believed he was invincible.

The legal documents drawn up after the divorce gave his parents custody of the boys in the event of his death. Would Dad really agree to raise two little boys? Would Shay want him to? What if Monica or her parents put up a fight?

Stop. You're delirious. It didn't happen. Every-thing's fine. He flopped onto his right side and stared at the wall.

Eventually he gave up on sleep and got up as the first light of dawn illuminated the space between the curtains and the window.

After breakfast, Shay dragged through the morning routine, responding to questions with curt, monosyllabic answers. They were scheduled to wash the fire engines after breakfast and roll call. Good. He could handle that.

"Dude, can I get you another cup of coffee?" Hamilton brushed past him and grabbed a sponge from the shelf on the garage wall. "I know it was a long night, but you are in a foul mood."

"I don't need more coffee." Gritting his teeth, Shay filled a bucket with soap and water.

"Campbell, don't you have a committee meeting this morning?" The chief joined them in the parking lot.

Warmth crept up Shay's neck. That's right. Natalie had rescheduled the meeting. He vaguely recalled reading the brief email. "Yes, sir."

"Come by my office when you're finished. I'd like a progress report."

Shay nodded. "I will."

Trent waited until the chief was out of earshot and then turned to Shay, his eyes gleaming. "Make sure you update him on your progress with the committee chairperson."

"Shut it." Shay aimed the hose at him.

"Yep, you're right, Hamilton." Trent jumped out of the way as water sprayed the asphalt near his feet. "He's testy."

"Thank you for coming." Natalie let her gaze slide around the table, first to Missy and then Shay, careful not to linger on his crisp uniform or his lips. No, definitely not his lips. She'd noted, with a small amount of satisfaction, the dark circles under his eyes. At least she wasn't the only one losing sleep this week. "I'll give Pastor Adams a few more minutes to get here. Maybe something came up."

The door to Coffee at the Corner swung open, and two young moms came in, babies wrapped against their chests.

"I drove by the house on my way here. The roof looks amazing." Missy's curly hair bounced as she talked, her wide smile like a beacon of light slicing through the sullen vibes emanating from Shay's side of the table. Other than a brief hello when he sat down, he hadn't said one word.

"Yes, we've made so much progress. Still miles to go, though." Natalie reached for her water. "Hopefully the windows and siding will be next."

Shay leaned one elbow on the table, propping his chin in his palm. Maybe she should ask the chief to assign someone else to the committee.

She sipped her water, the cool liquid coating her suddenly parched throat.

"May I give an update on the trucks and heavy equipment like we talked about last time?" Missy asked, her smile fading as she cast an uncertain look in Shay's direction.

"Please do." At least somebody wanted to talk.

"My husband spoke with his manager, who has a friend with a big equipment rental place on Capital Boulevard. Anyway, we've lined up several trucks for the festival. A cement mixer, a backhoe, a bobcat…" She ticked each one off on her fingers. "What am I forgetting? Oh, an articulating dump truck." Her smile returned. "I'm so pumped. Shay, don't you have little boys? I bet they're totally into stuff like this."

"Excuse me?" Shay lifted his head. "Oh, yeah. Trucks. Right."

Was he even listening? Before she could ask him, a text message chimed on her phone.

"I'm sorry. Let me see who this is." She glanced at the screen. "Pastor Adams is visiting someone in the hospital and can't get away." Flipping her phone over to avoid any more distractions, she wrote his name on her notepad and circled it as a reminder to follow-up later. "I'll email him an update. No worries."

"How about the fire department? Still on for the usual fire safety spiel?" There. If he wouldn't talk to her, she'd draw him in with direct questions. He couldn't ignore her forever.

"Absolutely." Shay's green eyes skimmed hers and then darted away again.

Squirming in her seat, she checked her notes once more. They hadn't seen each other since they'd kissed. He had every right to be upset with her, but did he have to be so…passive? She'd try a new tactic. "Please let the guys at the station know we're so grateful for everything they've done."

"We're happy to help." The terseness in his voice said quite the opposite. He'd probably rather have a root canal than sit here another minute.

"I don't want to keep you any longer. I'm sure you both have plenty to do. The festival is coming together. Janeanne, from the community center, is coordinating the booths. She'll have prizes for the kids. I've talked Erin into finding volunteers to provide pies for the pie-eating contest. Jayce Philips's mom left me a voice mail yesterday, and we're still on for the concert. He—"

"Have you heard his new song on the radio?" Missy splayed her hands across her chest. "I'm a happily married woman, but his voice—it's incredible."

Shay groaned and rolled his eyes.

Missy shot him another confused glance. "What? What did I say?"

Natalie couldn't stop the laughter bubbling from her lips. "Don't let him fool you. He doesn't want anyone else to know, but he told me he already downloaded the song. Missy, I think we're looking at Jayce Philips's biggest fan."

If looks could kill, she'd be writhing on the floor.

"Do you not like him?" Missy fiddled with the pendant hanging around her neck. "You know he grew up here, right?"

"I've never met the guy. I hear only good things about him. Country music doesn't impress me." Shay glanced at his watch. "If we're finished here…"

So much for adding levity to the situation. He obviously wasn't interested in jokes. Or any conversation, for that matter. She hated that things were so messy and complicated between them. If he left before she had a chance to apologize for her behavior the other day, things would continue to fester.

Here goes nothing.

"Actually, if I could speak with you for a minute, Shay?"

He hesitated, half standing as he moved to push back his chair.

Missy took the hint. "I've got to run. My daughter has a dentist appointment in Raleigh."

"Thanks again for your help, Missy." Natalie waved as her friend grabbed her purse and slid from her seat. "I'll see you later."

Shay stood, already angled halfway toward the door.

More than one set of curious eyes looked their direction from nearby tables. Natalie scooped up her belongings and shoved them inside her handbag. "Could we talk outside?"

"I've really got to get back to work."

"Please. It's important."

He nodded. "I'll follow you out."

Erin winked as Natalie passed the front counter. "Have a great day, y'all."

"You, too." She forced a smile, knowing full well she'd be back to give her friend an instant replay of the conversation once Shay left.

Outside, she moved a safe distance from the shop's entrance, her heart in her throat as she composed her muddled thoughts.

"Are you going to walk me back to the station?"

Natalie stopped near the pair of large terra-cotta containers separating the walkway from the parking lot. The red-and-yellow mums Erin had planted swayed in the cool breeze. Turning, she squared her shoulders. "I don't want to have this conversation with half the coffee shop spectating."

He linked his arms across his chest. "I'm not sure I want to have this conversation at all."

"Please. Hear me out. I need to apologize."

"Keep talking."

He was not going to make this easy, was he? "I'm sorry I ran off."

Shay studied her, his probing stare undermining her shaky composure. "Is that it?"

"What do you mean?"

The subtle lift of his shoulders seemed anything

but casual. "You dragged me out here like you were going to pour your heart out. I was expecting something a little more...profound."

What was wrong with her? She pinched the bridge of her nose with her fingers. She couldn't even apologize without messing up. "I'm sorry— that didn't come out the way I'd planned." Her heart kicked against her ribs. Maybe she needed to tell him everything. Starting with the offer from Forever Love.

"Here's the thing." Shay scuffed the toe of his work boot against the asphalt. "I care about you, Natalie. I've had fun getting to know you, and I can't wait to go to the festival and see a deserving family receive this house we're all working hard to finish."

She dropped her hand to her side, mindful of all he didn't say. "But?"

"As much as I enjoyed our first kiss, I don't want to take you away from what you truly value. You've made it clear that the needs of your family come first, and I respect your decision. My boys are certainly my first priority, too. Maybe it's best if you and I are just friends."

She swallowed hard. "Friends. Right. Because we both need to put our families first." Parroting his words back to him did nothing to ease the painful ache forming in her chest.

"I'm glad we both agree on what matters most."

He gave her forearm a gentle squeeze. "I'll see you around."

He released his grip, offered a half smile that didn't quite reach his eyes and then pulled out his keys and jogged toward the fire department vehicle parked a few spaces away.

She stood alone, already missing the warmth of his fingertips brushing her skin. If this is what it meant to follow her dreams, why did she feel so empty?

After his grueling shift, Shay craved some quality time with Aiden and Liam. Too bad his thoughts kept returning to his conversation with Natalie outside the coffee shop. He shook his head, determined to compartmentalize his muddled emotions and focus on the logical facts. By her own admission, she had a lot going on. So did he. Telling her they'd be better off as friends was the right decision. Wasn't it? Somebody needed to say it, since she obviously felt their kiss was a mistake. But as soon as the words left his lips, and the hurt flashed in her eyes, he wanted to snatch them back. If they agreed friendship was best, why did he feel so disappointed?

He slowed to a stop in front of his house, frowning at the delivery truck backed up to the garage.

"Child's Play," he whispered, studying the company's name and the picture of playground equipment decorating the truck's side panel. There must be some mistake. Maybe they had the wrong house. He certainly hadn't ordered anything like that.

Grabbing his duffle bag from the passenger seat, he got out and walked up his driveway. In this age of GPS and smartphones, it seemed odd that they couldn't find the right address. He stopped and peeked in the window on the driver's side. The cab was empty. Surely Mom hadn't invited them in?

Aiden and Liam's familiar squeals and the hum of men's voices floated from the backyard. What in the world? His pulse sped as he rounded the side of the house and unlatched the gate.

His father stood in the middle of the yard, talking with two young men in jeans and polo shirts. Mom stood near the concrete slab by the back door, laughing as the boys chased inflatable beach balls around.

"Mom?" Shay dropped his bag in the grass. "What's going on?"

Aiden spotted him first. "Dada!"

"Daddy!" Liam barreled past his brother, set on a direct course for Shay.

"There he is." Dad turned around, a smile brightening his normally stern features. "Surprise. Did you know you were getting a new swing set today?"

Shay kneeled in the grass and braced for impact as Liam and Aiden pounced. "You're kidding, right?"

Mom crossed the lawn to meet him, tugging the hem of her gingham blouse over her blue jeans.

"What in the—"

"I know." She patted his shoulder. "I'm as surprised as you are. But once your father gets an idea in his head, there's no arguing."

"Really? It's my yard. The boys aren't ready for a swing set. I'm not ready."

"Daddy, play." Aiden tugged on Shay's arm.

"In a minute, buddy." Shay stood up. "Why don't you go get your ball?"

"They'll grow into it." Mom's eyes pleaded. "With the weather turning cooler, this is the ideal time to play outside."

"We have a great park with a playground, right down the street. And an entire farm less than a half mile away."

"Dada, up, up." Liam clung to him. Shay swung him up onto his shoulders. Liam tunneled his fingers through Shay's hair.

"What do you think?" Dad strolled over and offered a glossy brochure. "This outfit is top notch."

Ignoring the advertisement, Shay tightened his grip on Liam's legs nestled against his chest. "You should've asked me first."

Dad's tight smile faded. "It's a gift, from your mother and me."

"That's a rather substantial gift."

The guys who'd come with the truck exchanged nervous glances.

"Consider it birthday and Christmas all rolled into one."

"It's almost October. Their birthdays were in August."

Dad rubbed a hand over his salt-and-pepper crew cut. "If we waited until Christmas, it would be too cold for them to enjoy it."

"Sweetie, you begged us for a swing set when you were a kid." Mom nudged the beach ball with her toe, and Aiden went after it.

That was true. Disappointed with the lame playground near their house at the military base, he'd campaigned hard for installing one in their own tiny yard. Dad must have anticipated his orders for his next assignment overseas, because he'd nixed the idea immediately. A few months later, Shay moved to the boarding school.

"Sir, if you're concerned about safety, I can assure you we're selling a quality product." One of the guys moved closer. "It's a custom design with—"

"Hold on." Shay held up his hand. "You bought a custom-made swing set?"

"Of course." Dad rocked back on his heels. "Nothing but the best for our grandsons."

Shay huffed out a short laugh.

Dad's expression hardened. "What's so funny?"

"Kind of ironic, isn't it? You've hardly paid any attention to them since we've moved here. Then you show up with a fancy play structure."

Tucking the brochure under his arm, Dad fixed

Shay with an icy stare. "Maybe if you had something for these boys to do out here, your mother wouldn't have to work so hard to keep them occupied."

"So, watching my boys is too much work?" He glanced at Mom. "Is this true?"

Mom moistened her lips. "Your father is concerned I'm overdoing it. But you know how much I love them, and I'm always happy to help."

"Belinda, your knees have been hurting for weeks."

"Warren, my knees have bothered me for months. It has nothing to do with Liam and Aiden."

Mom's knees hurt? Why didn't she tell him? Shay lifted Liam from his shoulders and placed him on the grass. "Go play with your brother while I talk to Grandpa, please."

Liam toddled off in pursuit of Aiden and his beach ball.

"Dad, if you're concerned about how much time Mom is spending here, then let me know, and I'll make other arrangements. I've offered numerous times to hire a nanny."

"That will cost you an absolute fortune." Mom planted her fists on her hips. "There's no need to do something so drastic."

From the corner of his eyes, Shay saw Aiden flop on his tummy across a beach ball. Anticipating what would happen next, Shay moved to intervene. "Aiden, be care—"

The ball popped out from under him, and Aiden did a face+plant in the grass. Liam giggled, attempting to mimic Aiden's trick with the ball.

"You okay, buddy?" Shay reached for him, but Aiden pushed himself to his feet and chased after the ball again.

"See?" Shay faced his parents. "They can barely handle a beach ball, much less a climbing wall, swings, monkey bars. What happens when they fall?"

"They dust themselves off and try again." Dad pulled out the brochure, tapping it against his palm. "I'm offering to build them a toy, not hand them the keys to a Ferrari."

Shay's pulse pounded in his ears. "I don't understand why you think this is a good idea. Look at that platform next to the slide." He jabbed his finger at the glossy picture. "That's easily a six-foot drop to the ground. There's no way that's safe for a two-year-old."

"Then we'll block that off until they're bigger. You've got to give them some freedom to be little boys. They'll figure out their own limits. You don't need to hover so much."

He'd heard enough. "Don't you get it? I can't afford not to hover."

Dad's expression paled. "Is this about—"

"I can't do this." Shay brushed past him. "Please tell your crew to leave. You're not putting that thing in my yard. Aiden, Liam, it's time to go inside."

His anger spiked as he herded the boys through the back door. No matter how many years passed, the memory of that horrible day came roaring back when he least expected.

"Don't hover," he grumbled under his breath. Easy for Dad to say. He'd coped by eliminating the problem—shipping Shay off to boarding school. Crisis resolved.

You don't get it, Dad. It's never that simple. He'd continue to hover. It was his responsibility to protect these precious lives entrusted to his care. Because he never again wanted to experience the kind of pain that ripped their family apart when his brother died.

Chapter Nine

Natalie sat in her home office on Thursday afternoon, staring at the clock on her computer screen. The time was 12:58 p.m. Butterflies fluttered in her abdomen. In two minutes, she'd have the most important phone call of her professional career—the scheduled video conference with the owners of Forever Love.

She took a sip of water from the bottle on her desk to ease the dry-as-cotton sensation in her mouth.

Deep breaths. You've got this.

Lingering doubts had plagued her, keeping her awake past midnight as she analyzed the pros and cons of her decision. What if she said yes and Daddy became gravely ill? Would she have to turn around and move back to Meadow Springs? Or would her financial support be enough? If she said no to Forever Love, would a better opportunity come along later?

Shay's green eyes intruded on her thoughts. She frowned. Not quite the opportunity she had in mind. The familiar chime of an incoming call sent her heart into her throat.

She clicked on the green icon to accept the call and willed her lips to form a convincing smile that masked her uncertainty. "Good morning. This is Natalie."

A woman in her midfifties, with a sleek, auburn bob and a flawless porcelain complexion, appeared on Natalie's computer screen. "Hi, Natalie. I'm Penny Winslow, Karen's partner at Forever Love." Penny smiled, revealing perfectly aligned teeth. "It's a pleasure to meet you."

"It's nice to meet you, too." Natalie sat up straighter, wishing she'd chosen bolder accessories or a more sophisticated outfit, instead of her understated black blazer over a simple black sheath. "I've always enjoyed weddings I've attended at Forever Love's venues."

"I'm glad to hear that. If all goes according to plan, we hope you'll be coordinating events at those venues very soon." Penny's confident declaration sent another jolt of adrenaline through Natalie's body. Had they already assumed she'd say yes?

"Thank you for speaking with me today," Penny said. "Unfortunately Karen can't join us. She's managing a crisis regarding one of Saturday's weddings."

"I understand." Natalie adjusted the desk chair

to get a better angle with her computer's camera. "I'm flattered you and Karen are interested in acquiring Magnolia Lane."

"Are you kidding? Karen can't stop talking about that barn. And your portfolio is stunning. Rustic yet elegant—the ideal asset in a wedding venue these days."

Yes! Natalie folded her hands in her lap to resist pumping the air with her fist. "Thank you. My family and I worked very hard to restore the livery to its current condition."

"It's beautiful." Penny touched the strand of pearls dangling around her neck. "Just to clarify, your family is on board with the sale of Magnolia Lane to an outside firm?"

Natalie's stomach clenched. *Haven't exactly mentioned it yet.* She willed her polite smile not to waver while she formulated a coherent response. "I own the barn and the two-acre plot. It was given to me by my grandparents."

"Oh, good. That makes the logistics of the barn becoming one of our venues simpler." Papers rustled, and Penny glanced down. "I can't emphasize enough how excited we are that you're considering joining our team. Are there any questions or concerns I can address this morning?"

"There hasn't been any mention of a quota. My hope is that joining your firm would allow me to focus on my strengths and channel my energy into my true passion, which is planning exquisite weddings. I'm accustomed to handling about sixty to seventy events per year, and I'm wondering if I'm expected to coordinate more or less than that as a member of Forever Love's staff?"

"Excellent question. Initially, we'll provide extensive hands-on training and orientation. You'll be taking direction from Karen and me and assisting with events in the Charlotte-area venues. If all goes well, after three to four months, you'll coordinate events on your own. Two weddings a week isn't unheard of."

Oh. Natalie hesitated. She hadn't anticipated a probationary period. What about the weddings here? "The contract clearly states you're acquiring my business, and that I'll be expected to work with clients in a variety of venues, which makes total sense, especially as I transition into the new role. I—I guess I assumed I'd still be the point person for any events booked at Magnolia Lane. Particularly events that I've already scheduled for next year."

Penny offered a tight smile. "We value what you bring to the table, Natalie, including your existing clients and future bookings. Of course we'll consider your insights regarding Magnolia Lane and future events."

"I see." Natalie tried to dismiss the uncertainty Penny's response provoked. It would be good for her to relinquish control of "her" barn to another team member, right? And Forever Love had a stellar reputation. "I'm sure any bride would be thrilled to have an event planner from Forever Love at the helm of the biggest day of her life."

"We like to think so," Penny said. "Since you've mentioned your existing client base, and your portfolio speaks for itself, why are you willing to consider this opportunity?"

Natalie's gaze drifted to the framed photo of her family propped on the edge of her desk. They'd all posed in front of the new tractor, Mama and Daddy beaming as they held a banner on the farm's first official opening day. Had that really been ten years ago?

"Natalie?"

Penny's voice drew her back to the present. *Focus.*

"I'm not sure there is ever an ideal time to make a major life change. Planning weddings exclusively is my dream job, as opposed to juggling Magnolia Lane and managing our family's farm at the same time. One is always at the mercy of the demands of the other."

Penny nodded, her dark eyes filled with empathy.

"In terms of the bigger picture, the sale of Magnolia Lane to you will provide for my parents' long-term needs, allowing me to focus on the career I've always dreamed of. I feel this role definitely plays to my strengths."

"Excellent. This appears to be a mutually beneficial partnership. If you accept our offer."

"I hope so." The muscles knotted at the base of her neck loosened. Penny was right. This deal was a win-win. So why couldn't she shake the uncertainty and accept the offer?

Footsteps on Natalie's porch followed by a soft knock at the front door startled her. There's no way she'd answer that. Whoever it was would have to wait.

"Karen and I are so pleased with your knowledge and experience. I—"

"Nat? Are you in here?" Cami's voice echoed from the front room.

Natalie froze. Talk about lousy timing.

Penny arched one pencil-thin eyebrow. "Everything okay?"

"Yes. I'm so sorry. Please continue." She considered rolling her desk chair away from the computer and kicking the office door shut, but that seemed unprofessional.

"It sounds like you have another appointment. Why don't you take another week to consider our offer? I sense some uncertainty about what this means for your venue, and I want you to be sure you're making an informed decision."

Cami's footsteps moved closer. Natalie prayed she wouldn't pop her head inside the office.

"Oh. Um—okay. That's very generous of you. Thank you. If I accept, when would I start?"

"We'd love to have you on board before Christmas."

Natalie forced a smile. "Perfect."

So soon. Could she uproot her whole life and move away before the end of the year?

"Thank you for your time, Natalie. Take your time with this decision. Karen will give you a call sometime in the next few weeks, and you can give us a definitive answer. Selfishly, I hope it's a yes."

"Thank you very much."

"Take care." Penny disconnected the call.

Natalie turned off the camera and sagged against the back of the chair.

"Who was that?"

Her heart lurched, and she spun around. Cami stood in the doorway, fists on her hips. "Cami, what in the world? Why are you here?" Was Clemson on fall break already?

"I just got here. Was that a job interview?"

"Why are you eavesdropping?"

"Answer the question. You're interviewing for a new job, aren't you?"

Natalie brushed a piece of lint from her skirt and dragged her gaze to meet Cami's. "Not exactly. More of a…merger."

"A merger?" Cami's eyes widened. "When were you planning to tell us? After you accepted the deal?"

"I haven't accepted anything. She made an offer, and now she followed up with an extension. I—I need more time to think about it."

"Is this why you were so mad at Tisha for the

solar energy thing? Because it messed with your secret plans to sell the barn?"

Natalie glared. "This is exactly why I didn't tell you anything yet, because I knew you'd overreact."

Hurt flashed in Cami's eyes. "I'm not overreacting."

"Fine. You're not overreacting." Natalie sighed. "I'm thinking of selling Magnolia Lane to Forever Love. They've offered me a job in Charlotte."

Cami sucked in a breath.

"Since you all are so content to let somebody else do the work around here," Natalie continued, "I guess one of you will need to step up."

"We're not content to *let* you do the work—we thought you were happy in your role. You've never asked for help, so how are we supposed to know?"

Natalie stopped short of rolling her eyes. "Look around. Who was I going to ask? You've all left."

"Because you led us to believe you were happy. If you hate it so much, why did you open Magnolia Lane?"

She pressed her palms to her face. *Don't you get it?* Dropping her hands to her sides, she met Cami's gaze again. "Seeing the families spend time together at the farm, and knowing they'll come back again and again—that we're a part of their traditions—it's very rewarding. But I love planning weddings more than I like coordinating pumpkin patch visits and holiday light displays. Saying yes to Forever Love's offer means saying yes to what

I've always wanted—a role as a wedding planner for one of North Carolina's most prestigious firms. This is an incredible opportunity for me, Cam. How can I say no to the job of my dreams?"

Cami's eyes welled with tears. "It makes me sad that you didn't care enough to share any of that with us."

"It makes me sad that none of you ever cared enough to ask."

"Ducks, ducks." Aiden and Liam scampered around Shay's legs, bumping into the other customers waiting in line, their voices getting louder with each passing second.

"Hold on a second, please." Shay tucked his wallet into the back pocket of his jeans, collected his tickets from the girl working the admissions counter and then followed the boys through the gated entrance. No matter how many times he told himself he'd find another activity to enjoy with them besides the farm, all they had to do was ask, and he'd give in.

"Ducks? Race?" Liam pointed to the water troughs and hand pumps nearby. "Please?"

"Sure, we can give it a try." He stole a quick glance toward the pond and gazebo. Even though he'd told Natalie they should only be friends, it didn't stop him from wishing they'd cross paths. So coming to the farm wasn't only for the boys' benefit. He'd play with rubber ducks all day long if it meant a chance to see her again.

"Daddy, help." Aiden strained to reach a rubber duck floating in the water trough.

"No. Me, me." Liam tapped his chest, clambering to move his brother out of the way.

"Easy, boys. We can all work together on this one."

He might as well have been talking to himself. Aiden and Liam both grabbed the metal handle for the water pump at the same time, screeching in frustration when neither one would let go. Aiden pushed Liam out of the way, knocking him off balance. He landed on his backside in a mud puddle, his eyes filling with tears.

"No, sir." Shay clasped Aiden's shoulder firmly and tugged him aside. "That's not how we treat one another."

Reaching down, Shay helped Liam to his feet and brushed most of the mud from the back of his shorts. "You're all right. It'll dry soon."

With a determined look on his little face, Liam made a valiant attempt at grabbing the pump handle.

Aiden would have none of it. He broke free from Shay's grasp and piled his hands on top of Liam's. "No, no, no," he wailed.

Shay blew out a long breath. "Seriously, boys? There's four pumps here, and you both have to have that one?"

Guiding Liam to the next pump, Shay gave the handle a few quick cranks. The rubber duck rode the wave of water down the narrow trough. Liam grinned, clapping his hands with delight.

"No, Daddy, no. Me, me." Aiden stomped his foot as he clutched two rubber ducks in his tiny fists.

"Hey, y'all. Are you having a good time?"

The sound of Natalie's voice calmed his frayed nerves. Shay pivoted and found her standing behind him, looking quite attractive in jeans, boots and a blue sweater that matched her eyes.

"Hey." He gestured to the boys. "Your duck race is a huge hit with the two-year-old crowd."

"Yeah, I get that a lot." She stretched out her hand toward Liam. "Hey, buddy. Want me to help you? Maybe our duck could race your Dad and brother's duck. Doesn't that sound fun?"

Liam studied her as if he couldn't quite decide what to make of her offer. Then he took her hand and walked with her to the next water pump. "Oh, good. I'm so glad you're here to help me." She gave Shay a smile that made his insides do crazy things.

"On the count of three, we all start pumping. The first duck to the other end of the trough wins." She waited while Liam found a duck he liked and placed it in the water.

"Are you guys ready, Aiden?" Natalie's prompt reminded Shay he'd been standing there, enamored –

with her ability to redirect Liam, when he should've been prepping for their race.

"Oh, right." He manned the pump with Aiden's hands on his and forced himself to focus on the duck and not Natalie's playful smile.

"Okay, on my count. One, two, three. Go!" she yelled.

Shay and Aiden pushed and pulled the handle, and spurts of water propelled their rubber ducks toward the finish line.

"Come on, Liam," Natalie cheered, her pump handle squealing in protest. "We can do this."

"Let's go, Aiden." He pumped harder, keeping an eye on Natalie and Liam's progress.

At the last second, Natalie and Liam's duck surged ahead and toppled off the trough and into the bin at the other end.

"Great job, buddy." She scooped Liam up and twirled him around. "We did it."

Liam tipped his face to the sky, giggling as he clutched the sleeves of her sweater. Shay's heart expanded at the sheer joy on Liam's face and Natalie's willingness to jump in and play. Didn't she know how much she meant to them already? How much she meant to him?

Banishing that thought, he shifted his focus to Aiden. Certain there would be tears over losing the race, he reached for the little boy.

"More?" Aiden glanced up at him for approval.

"Sure, we can race again." Natalie set Liam on the ground. "How about we go two out of three?"

"What's the prize?"

She grinned. "Bragging rights, I suppose. Or how about a train ride?"

"We didn't pay for admission to the train ride."

"No worries. I have connections." Her gaze held his, and for one glorious instant, the boys and their petty squabbles melted away.

"Train?" Aiden dropped the duck and trotted off in the direction of the train.

"Wait." Shay caught up with him before he collided with a woman pushing a stroller.

"We don't have to race the ducks anymore." Natalie fell in step beside him with Liam clinging to her hand. "If they'd rather ride the train, I can take you right now."

"Might be best." Shay held up his hands in mock surrender. "I know you were looking forward to beating us a second time, but I don't think Aiden could take it."

"Aiden couldn't take it?" She nudged him with her hip. "Or Aiden's dad couldn't?"

"Are you implying that I'm a sore loser?"

"I wouldn't say 'sore' exactly." Laughter crept into her smile. "How about highly competitive?"

He couldn't suppress his own smile. "I don't like to lose. Not even a rubber duck race."

"Well, I hate to break it to you, but there's nothing to win on this train ride. The seats are all the same. We let you ride long enough to see the whole farm twice, so no one can complain they didn't get a good view of everything."

"That's fine. I hope you'll allow a safety-related question?"

Uncertainty flickered in her gaze. "Just one."

"Are there seat belts? I could use some adult conversation, and strapping these two in is my only hope."

She tilted her head, eyes gleaming. "No seat belts, I'm afraid. But I think they'll be sufficiently distracted by the scenery."

Me, too. His pulse skittered at the bold thought. *C'mon, man. Enough with the flirting. What happened to just friends?*

Liam and Aiden spotted the train pulling into the boarding area and tugged Natalie and Shay to the platform.

"Slow down, fellas. We're not going to miss anything." Shay hustled to corral Aiden before he squeezed between someone's legs and forced his way through the crowd.

"I could get us to the front of the line, but I think all these people would hate me. And I'd kind of like for them to stick around and enjoy the rest of the farm."

"No, don't make a scene. Besides, that sends the boys the wrong message."

"I was kidding."

"Oh." He grimaced. "Sorry. I thought you were offering the VIP treatment."

"Nope, none of that around here." She pointed to the fence separating them from the train track. "Boys, if you stand here, you can see the train coming back from the pumpkin patch."

Captivated, Aiden and Liam clung to the railing and peered through the opening between the slats. In the distance, the train chugged along, making a slow lap around the farm.

"This is pretty cool." Shay moved in behind the boys, standing watch in case they slipped and fell. "How did y'all decide to put in a train?"

Natalie laughed. "Well, it's not a real train, obviously. My uncle Bill saw something like it at the state fair and figured out what kind of a tractor we'd need, how many people it could tow without breaking down. Initially, we thought it was the craziest idea ever. Now it's one of the highlights for families and the destination experience."

"You've got to be one of the only pumpkin patches for miles around offering something like this."

"We're getting more competition from farms on the west side of Raleigh than we ever have before. But you're right. This is the only farm that I know of with a train ride."

"It's a sweet setup."

"Thanks." Her brow furrowed as she stared across the field.

"What's wrong?"

"Rough morning."

"I'm sorry to hear that. Do you want to talk about it?"

A mixture of emotions clouded her features. Warning bells sounded in his head. What was bothering her?

She kept her voice low. "I have to deal with some interpersonal conflict later, and I'm dreading it."

"Really."

Her manicured fingertips massaged her forehead. "It's not going to go well."

"How do you know?"

"I just do."

She sounded so sullen. Defeated. Before he could ask more questions, the train pulled up to the platform, its cars loaded with enthusiastic adults and children. They chattered and waved to the crowd waiting in line, while the driver—an older man dressed in the traditional engineer's uniform of navy-and-white pinstriped overalls and a matching cap—directed his passengers to unload safely.

Liam and Aiden backed away from the fence, their little bodies almost humming with anticipation as the train cars cleared out.

"Hold on, boys." Shay grabbed their hands before they could climb through the fence. "It's your turn next."

As promised, the line moved quickly, and they were soon settled on bench seats in one of the cars.

Shay claimed a spot next to Natalie, praying the boys could handle sitting together across from him.

"Will they be okay?" Natalie studied them.

Aiden and Liam sat scrunched against one wall of the car, holding hands in a rare display of solidarity.

"Let's give it a try." Shay resisted the temptation to slide his arm around her shoulders. "That whole adult conversation thing, remember?"

She didn't smile at his attempt at humor.

"Do you have to resolve this issue soon? Or could you give it some time?"

"That's the thing. One of my sisters overheard a phone conversation, and she was pretty upset. Now I feel cornered. If I don't follow through, she might do it for me. But I haven't worked up the courage to tell anyone else." She turned her troubled gaze toward him. "She also said some things that really stung, and I'm afraid she might be right."

Shay nodded. He wanted to help. That's what friends did, right? "What's that old saying? The truth hurts?"

Natalie's frown deepened, and she looked away.

Way to cheer her up, genius. She didn't need him stating the obvious.

The train eased forward, and their bodies shifted closer together with the increasing speed. He savored the sensation of her leg brushing against the length of his, their shoulders gently bumping against each other. Nothing about this scenario was helping his decision to just be friends.

"I hope they'll be open-minded about what I have to say, but I'm scared they'll be angry."

"Why?"

She hesitated. "They'll accuse me of being selfish."

"Do you think you're being selfish?"

Natalie rode in silence, picking at a loose thread on the hem of her sweater.

Regret pricked at Shay. Maybe he'd asked the wrong question.

When she spoke, her voice was strained. "After everything I've done to keep the farm going? No. I don't. Even though I'm offering a solution to a major dilemma, they won't see it that way. They'll think I'm desert—" She heaved a sigh. "Never mind. I've probably said too much already. I doubt you want to hear about my family drama."

Not true. He studied her. "I'm sorry this has happened. I'm not a big fan of interpersonal conflict, either."

He fisted his hands in his lap and resisted the urge to lace his fingers through hers. He wanted to tell her he'd do anything to help her navigate through this. But he couldn't. That wasn't his role.

Chapter Ten

"Can I ask you something?" Natalie tore a piece of blue painter's tape from the roll and smoothed it across the new window's metal frame.

"Sure." Erin pried the lid off a can of paint. "I haven't seen you since you left the coffee shop with Shay. What's going on there, by the way?"

"Nothing." It was the truth. But that didn't mean she hadn't wished for there to be something.

Between juggling her responsibilities at the farm and the building project, Claire's wedding reception and avoiding telling her family about Forever Love's offer, she'd had very little time to consider what she truly wanted. Or how she might respond with a counteroffer. The thought of a new role solely dedicated to wedding planning still filled her with excitement. No broken tractor, payroll or inventory to manage. But it also meant not seeing Shay and his boys anymore, either. Their time together at the duck races, and then on the train ride, was…wonderful. She smiled at the memory of Liam in her arms, giggling, after they'd won. They were a handful, but so adorable, too.

"Nat?" Erin waved a wooden stir stick in front of Natalie's face. "What did you want to ask me?"

"Do you and Derek ever argue about the future?"

"What do you mean?"

"Do you both agree on where you'll live? I know you don't have kids yet, but have you already figured out who will stay home with them? Or will you both work?"

"The first one's easy. Neither of us wants to leave Meadow Springs. He's happy coaching football and teaching. Plus our families are here. But the childcare issue…" She let out a low whistle. "That's a hot topic. And one of the reasons why we aren't ready to start a family."

"So how will you figure it out?"

"Pray." Erin dipped the stick into the paint can and gave it a good stir. "Keep working through it. Not have a newborn during football season, like, ever."

Natalie gave her friend a weak smile. "Y'all are gonna be great parents someday."

"Thanks. Emphasis on someday. In Derek's perfect world, I'll sell the coffee shop and take care of the kids full-time."

"That's not what you had in mind?"

"I can't imagine not having the shop. What's not to love about coffee? It brings the community together, provides a gathering place, gives event planners a place to flirt with firefighters—" She clapped her hand over her mouth, eyes dancing.

"Whatever." Natalie frowned. "I wasn't flirting."

"Sure you weren't. The chemistry between you two is amazing. Missy noticed, too, because she hightailed it out of there."

"Her daughter had a dentist appointment."

"Convenient." Erin rummaged in a plastic shopping bag until she pulled out a package of paint rollers. "What's all this talk about the future? Are you and the firefighter making plans I need to know about?"

"Not a chance." Tearing another piece of tape from the roll, she slapped it on the wall. She was probably imagining that something meaningful had happened between them on the train yesterday.

"No chance with a firefighter, or just not with that particular firefighter?"

She sighed. "For the longest time, I didn't want to even think about dating again, and certainly not someone whose life was in danger every time they were on shift. But lately I've wondered if that isn't unrealistic."

"I can understand why you're being cautious. On the other hand, Spencer wouldn't expect you not to fall in love again," Erin said softly.

"I know." Natalie smoothed her hand along the strip of tape. "I don't want to be single forever."

There. She'd finally admitted it out loud. Those

sweet little boys and their handsome father had completely turned her world upside down—in the best kind of way.

"Nat? Did you hear me?"

"Sorry." Warmth crept up her neck. "I was distracted."

"Look at you, all worked up and we've barely mentioned him. Girl, you've got it bad."

"I do not."

Erin craned her neck. "If there's anything else you want to tell me, you'd better hurry up."

"Why?"

"Because here he comes."

Natalie whirled around. Sure enough, Trent and Shay walked up the driveway. The roll of tape slid from her hands. She flattened her back against the wall, her pulse quickening as she mentally gauged the distance to the sliding glass door off the future master bedroom across the hall. Could she make it before he came inside?

Smirking, Erin shook her head. "Don't even think about leaving. This butter yellow is all you, and I'm not painting this room by myself."

"It's a neutral color for a nursery." She wiped her sweaty palms on her jeans and recovered the roll of tape. Erin was right. This project needed her attention. They'd never finish on time if they didn't work together—the guys from the station were an essential factor in the equation. Even with their help, she wasn't confident the house would be ready in less than a month.

"Anybody here?" Shay's voice echoed through the front room.

"We're in the back," Erin called out, pouring paint into the metal tray at her feet.

"Hey." Trent leaned against the door frame, his gaze traveling around the small space. "How's it going?"

"Good morning. Perfect timing." Erin gestured to the rollers and brushes still lying on the floor. "We were just saying we could use some help. Especially with the tape. Natalie is taking forever."

Natalie shot her a look.

Shay crossed the room, joining her beside the window, his aftershave teasing her senses. "I could finish taping off the ceiling if you want."

"No, thanks. I'm almost done." She flashed a polite smile, and then she turned back to the task at hand. Those amazing eyes—green like rare sea glass—would not convince her to change her mind.

"I admire your optimism, but one wall out of four isn't exactly the same as done."

She ignored the teasing tone and slapped the tape down a little harder. Couldn't he find something else to do? There was a whole house to work on, and he had to be right here? Next to her?

"We'd gladly work on something else, if you point us in the right direction. How about the flooring?" Shay unfolded the ladder.

Groaning inwardly, Natalie passed the roll of tape to Shay. "Back-ordered."

"No way." Erin frowned. "How did that happen?"

"Apparently the order was never processed. Since the vendor is donating the product, I couldn't exactly complain."

"So what are you going to do?" Erin attached a roller to a long handle and gave it to Trent.

"I'm praying it comes through in time. If not, I'll come up with a plan B."

Natalie stilled, the brush in midair, paint dripping onto the toe of her sneaker. Had she bothered to pray about any of the issues she'd wrestled with lately? If she didn't quit relying on her own strength, she was going to overlook an essential detail. Something important would slip through the cracks and cause a crisis not even she could resolve. Her scalp prickled. This afternoon, she'd make time for solitude. Time for prayer. She certainly couldn't keep going at this pace.

The ladder creaked under Shay's boots as he climbed down. "The tape's finished. Mind if I help you paint?"

"Grab a brush." Natalie shifted the paint can closer. "That's one thing we have plenty of."

"I'll start cutting in around the window."

"Great."

They could do this—paint side by side and pretend like nothing ever happened between them.

Friends helped each other out in their time of need, right?

Trent and Erin fell into easy conversation about the high school football team, speculating about their chances for winning Friday night's game. Natalie stole a quick glance at Shay. A lock of his blond hair spilled across his forehead as he spread paint along the new drywall surrounding the window, his tongue wedged against his upper lip.

Stop. This would be the world's sloppiest paint job if she didn't get her act together. Maybe she should find something else to do. She inched away, wishing she didn't have to work so hard to concentrate with his arm occasionally bumping up against hers. When they both turned back to reload their brushes, knuckles grazing, Shay hesitated, his eyes searching her face.

"Sorry." She scooted back, giving him plenty of space.

"You don't have to be sorry." His mouth curved up in a smile.

Oh, but I am. She longed to tell him she wished things were different. That she was dragging her feet preparing her counteroffer for Forever Love, and he topped the list of reasons why. But she couldn't have this conversation here. Not now.

"How are the boys?" Swiping the excess paint from her brush on the edge of the can, she resumed her work, vowing to be more diligent. Aiden and Liam were always a safe topic. Surely she could ask about them and paint this wall. As long as she didn't slip and mention how often she thought about their chubby faces and contagious belly laughs.

"They've had better days. My mom's, um, taking some time off. I hired a new nanny, and today's her first day."

Poor little guys. "That's a big change."

"It is."

"How did you find your nanny?"

"There's a service that provides caregivers. They handle the interviews, background checks—all the prerequisites. This girl's a student at NC State, so she can't work full-time, but today seemed as good as any to give it a trial run."

"Do Liam and Aiden like her?"

"Not yet. I told her if they didn't stop crying by lunch to give me a call." He set down his brush and checked his phone. "No news is good news, I guess."

"Hey, Shay, I meant to tell you," Trent said, interrupting their conversation. "I checked with Caroline about those dates you mentioned. We have company coming, so we can't watch the boys. Sorry, man."

"Thanks, anyway. I'll figure something out."

Natalie studied the stiffness in his shoulders and the muscle working in his jaw. It couldn't be easy, planning childcare around shifts at the station. How much time off did his mother need?

"Is there anything I can do to help?"

Shay didn't mask his surprise. "You have time to watch Liam and Aiden for two days?"

"If I can plan a wedding and manage a farm, I'm pretty sure I can—"

"Natalie?" Kirsten yelled, her voice tinged with panic.

"Kirsten?" Natalie abandoned her brush and crossed the room in quick strides. Why did she sound so upset?

Footsteps pounded down the hall.

Moments later, Kirsten collided with her in the doorway, chest heaving and tears filling her eyes. "I'm so glad you're here."

Natalie clutched Kirsten's forearms with both hands. "What's going on? You're scaring me."

"It's Daddy. I went with him and Mama to the neurologist this morning."

Natalie squeezed her eyes closed. That appointment was today. She'd missed it. How could she forget?

"What did he say?" she whispered.

"The progression might be faster than we thought." Kirsten's voice broke. "He slurred a few of his words in front of the doctor and admitted he's started choking on his food. Mama's terrified. Lou Gehrig's disease shows no mercy, Nat. It's awful already. What are we going to do when things get really bad?"

I don't know. The uncertainty loomed over them like an ominous storm cloud as they stood in the hallway, clinging to one another and crying. How could she even think about leaving them at a time like this?

Shay hovered near the floral section at the grocery store, a half-gallon of chocolate peanut butter ice cream tucked under his arm. Was this really a good idea? He'd heard the chilling words and mention of Lou Gehrig's disease as Natalie and her sister stood in the house earlier. The whispers and the crying were impossible to ignore. He'd pretended to mind his own business and kept painting, while Erin intervened, ushering the girls back to the farm. Natalie's obvious distress bothered him, though. Erin insisted his plan to drop by with Natalie's favorite comfort food and fresh flowers was perfect, but now his confidence wavered. Maybe she'd rather be left alone. Didn't families circle the proverbial wagons in times like this?

Recalling the many friends he thought would call on him in his darkest hour and didn't, he selected a bouquet and then got in line to check out. The risk was worth it. He couldn't stand the thought of her suffering alone. A quick text from the new nanny confirmed the boys had finally gone down for their naps. He'd swing by Natalie's, deliver the flowers and ice cream, and still be home before they woke up.

On the short drive to the farm, Shay prayed the only words he could. *Please draw near to Nata-*

lie and her family, Lord. Comfort them. Surround them with people who will offer encouragement.

He gripped the steering wheel tighter, steadying the bouquet of flowers in the console with his free hand. No one he knew personally had Lou Gehrig's disease, but an internet search on his phone revealed a list of symptoms and complications that left a pit in his stomach. A difficult road lay ahead for the whole McDowell family.

He bypassed the entrance to the farm and then turned into Natalie's driveway. The aroma of kettle corn danced on the breeze, and dry leaves skittered across his path as he got out of his truck in front of Natalie's bungalow, which was situated on a small knoll near the pond. His pulse sped as he stood at the bottom of the steps, clutching the ice cream and flowers. The porch swing sat empty, and the blinds were drawn. Maybe she wasn't here. Or what if she answered, but told him to go away?

Don't overthink it.

He climbed the steps and gently tapped the brass knocker three times. Other than the distant, muted sound of children laughing, only silence answered back. Shifting his weight from one foot to the other, he glanced back over his shoulder. The McDowells' home sat at least fifty yards away, nestled in a grove of trees with a commanding view of the farm. There's no way he'd make an appearance there. If Natalie didn't come to the door, he'd leave the flowers and—

The door swung open.

"Shay?"

He pivoted and faced the doorway. Natalie stared at him, her eyes brimming with tears. Red splotches dotted her cheeks, and her messy ponytail fell across the shoulder of her faded Carolina T-shirt.

"I overheard your conversation about your dad. I'm so sorry." He extended the ice cream and flowers. "Thought these might help cheer you up."

Her face crumpled, and she pressed her fingertips to her mouth.

Oh, no. Didn't Erin say these were her favorites? "I'll go. Sorry to bother you. I'll leave these…" He lowered the carton to the welcome mat.

"Don't."

"Okay." Shay straightened, the plastic around the flowers crinkling in his sweaty hand.

"The flowers, the ice cream—it's all…" She dropped her chin to her chest, a fresh round of tears drowning out her words.

"I'm so sorry," he said again. The simple words would have to be enough. She'd made her feelings clear, and he had to honor their mutual decision, even though he longed to pull her into his arms and make the heartache go away.

She dragged the back of her hand across her cheeks.

"Here." Shay stepped inside, slid the flowers onto the table in the entryway, snatched a tissue from the box under the mirror and then handed it to her.

"Thanks." She sniffed, dabbing at the corners of her eyes. "Sorry I'm such a wreck."

"You don't need to apologize."

"Don't leave. Not yet. Please." She shook her head, forehead wrinkled. "Listen to me. I can't even form a coherent sentence."

"Why don't you sit down? I'll put the ice cream in the freezer if you want."

"Thank you." Her lower lip trembled. "I'll dive in later, once I pull myself together. The flowers are lovely, by the way. I can put those in water."

"Sit. I'll take care of it." He gripped her shoulders and steered her toward the sofa.

"There's a vase in the cabinet beside the sink."

"Excellent." He collected the ice cream and flowers and then gently closed the door.

Natalie padded across the hardwoods and settled into one corner of the overstuffed love seat. Shay glanced around. The tasteful furniture, warm colors and feminine touches were a refreshing change from his sparsely decorated, half-unpacked house.

Natalie was cocooned under a throw blanket, her legs drawn up beneath her. Shay clutched the cold carton tighter. The urge to circle around the end of the sofa and pull her back into his arms was almost overwhelming. *Flowers. Melting ice cream. Keep moving.*

In the kitchen, he stashed the carton in the freezer

and then frowned at the bouquet in his arms. Buying it was one thing. Arranging the flowers? Not so much. A pair of scissors rested in a slot on the knife block. Wasn't he supposed to trim the stems or something?

The cabinet closest to the sink held several vases on the top shelf, in addition to Natalie's impressive collection of pods for her single-serve coffee brewer. Apparently she had a strong affinity for tea, as well. He glanced over his shoulder. She'd slumped down, her head resting on the arm of the sofa. A hot drink might not be a bad idea. Setting a mug under the dispenser, he powered on the machine and popped a chamomile pod into the unit. While it brewed, he did a passable job of tucking the flowers into a tall crystal vase.

"Everything okay in there?" Natalie called out.

"Yep. One second." He left the vase in the middle of the granite countertop and slowly walked the steaming mug of tea back to the living room. A stack of coasters sat on a tray in the middle of the coffee table. He selected one and rested the mug on it.

"Would you like any cream or sugar?"

She gave a wobbly smile, her eyes coated in a fresh sheen of moisture. "It's perfect. Thank you."

"You're welcome." He inched away, his legs bumping against the table, suddenly self-conscious under her gaze.

"Would you sit with me?" she whispered.

He hesitated. Aiden and Liam would flip out if he wasn't there when they woke up. On the other hand, there were plenty of days when he was there for every single second. He could afford to sit with Natalie. Just for a few minutes.

He sank onto the end of the sofa. "Have you been to see your folks?"

She nodded, shifting to face him. "Erin walked Kirsten and me over to the house. I—I couldn't handle it. The place is crawling with people—relatives, church friends, Mama's garden club... It's overwhelming."

"Casseroles filling every square inch of counter space?"

She chuckled. "Yes. How did you know?"

He shrugged. "I'm a Southerner, too. I know how these things work."

"Thank you again for bringing the ice cream and flowers." She reached over and squeezed his hand, her fingers lingering on his. "That's very thoughtful."

The warmth of her touch jolted him, muddling his thoughts. He should go. Instead, he laced his fingers through hers. "You're welcome."

"How did the paint turn out?"

"Don't worry about the house, okay? It's all going to come together."

Tipping her head back, Natalie stared at the ceiling. "Asking me not to worry is like asking a thoroughbred not to run. It's what I do."

"Well...do less." He gave her hand a quick squeeze. "Focus on your family. Delegate tasks to all those people mingling in your parents' house right now."

A faint smile lifted one corner of her mouth as her eyelids fluttered closed. "I like the way you think."

"Thanks." *And I like you. A lot.*

He sat there far longer than he should have, listening to Natalie's deep, even breaths and wishing with all his heart he could erase her fears. Wishing that he'd never uttered the phrase "just friends."

Chapter Eleven

Natalie crept onto her parents' screened porch, easing the door closed behind her. The last few weeks had flown by in a blur, and the festival was two days away. Between scrambling to make sure the house was ready in time, and preparing her counteroffer, she barely had five minutes to spare. But she needed to stop by and see how her father was doing—how her whole family was coping.

"Good morning, Daddy."

"Hey, sweetheart." Daddy sat in the rocker in the corner, hands folded in his lap.

"It's chilly out here. Would you like a blanket?" She shivered as a light breeze rustled the golden leaves of the maple trees nearby. Sweatpants and a T-shirt weren't enough for him in this cooler weather.

"Will you pass me the one on the sofa, please? I'm waiting on your mama. She offered to bring me my breakfast." His eyes were clear and bright, while a smile turned up the corners of his mouth. "You're up early. What's the occasion?"

"I came to see about you." She handed him the faded red-and-blue quilt and then claimed the wicker rocker opposite his, perching on the edge of the tufted cushion. "How are you feeling?"

He stopped rocking and slowly draped the quilt around his shoulders. Often a man of few words, he seemed to measure them even more carefully now. "This disease is not something I would wish on anyone. It's difficult. I expect it will get harder. Giving it an official label doesn't change anything."

"What do you mean?"

"There's still a farm to run, decisions to be made. Now that your sisters are all here, we can have some frank discussions about the future."

Her throat tightened. "What kind of discussions?"

"I heard about—" Daddy pressed his fist to his mouth, a thick, watery cough overtaking him. As his face reddened, Natalie dug her fingernails into the ridges of the wicker armrests. Had Cami already told everyone about Forever Love's offer?

"Need some water?"

"No," he gasped. "Just a little cough."

"I wouldn't call that little." Peering through the back door, she searched for Mama in the kitchen. Shouldn't she be out here by now? Mama stood at the counter, spreading jelly on a slice of toast.

Natalie shifted back toward Daddy. The coughing fit had ceased, and his color looked sort of normal. *Now's your chance.* If she was going to tell him about selling Magnolia Lane, this might be her only opportunity. Once Mama and her sisters joined them, keeping his attention would be a losing proposition. And she couldn't have an honest conversation with her family about the future if they didn't know about Forever Love's offer. But pushing her agenda on the heels of a life-changing diagnosis felt…wrong. Her stomach gurgled, both from hunger and anxiety. When had she eaten last, anyway?

The door to the house swung wide, and Cami appeared, her hair in a messy topknot and an orange Clemson sweatshirt layered over her pajamas.

Natalie studied her sister, searching for any clues that she might've shared what she'd overheard in Natalie's office. "Good morning."

Cami settled on the wicker sofa. "Mornin'. What's new?"

"I came by to catch up, since everyone's here. Together."

"Yep." Cami glanced toward Daddy and back again. "We're all here. Trying to figure out what to do next."

"We don't have to figure it all out today," Daddy said quietly.

Cami yawned. "Want some coffee, Nat? Clearly I need some."

"I would love some coffee. Thank you."

"How about fixing a cup for Walt, too?" Daddy glanced at his watch. "He should be here any minute."

She stepped back, narrowly missing a collision with Mama. "Why?" Walt Frederickson, their family attorney, didn't make casual house calls, especially not before eight o'clock in the morning.

"Oh, it's a little early for shop talk, isn't it?" Mama lowered a tray with medication, toast and a cup of coffee onto the side table. "Your father needs breakfast first. He's got to keep his strength up."

"Talking to my family won't wear me out. The girls need to know what's going on." Daddy reached for the slice of toast, his hand trembling as he maneuvered it to his mouth.

Natalie pulled more chairs into a semicircle. Cami, Kirsten and Tisha came out, coffee mugs in hand.

"Here." Tisha passed one to Natalie, avoiding her gaze. "There's cream and sugar inside."

"Thank you." Natalie welcomed the warmth of the steaming mug against her hands. That was the most interaction they'd had since their ugly conversation at Magnolia Lane. She opened her mouth to say something more, but Tisha turned away and sank into the chair closest to Mama. Natalie took the hint and let Cami and Kirsten fill in the space between them. Maybe it was better this way. She and Tisha had never agreed on much, anyway.

"It's nice to have y'all here." Mama gripped Daddy's arm, her pale pink lips forming a sad smile. "I wish the circumstances were different."

"We're always happy to be home, Mama." Cami and Tisha exchanged glances.

Regret pricked at Natalie's heart. Could she really tell them that she planned to leave?

"Walt is dropping by for a visit on his way to a golf tournament. He's not here on official business or anything." Mama peeled a banana and handed it to Daddy. "Although, we are going to have to involve him in some of our more pressing decisions later, and make sure our wills are updated."

More pressing decisions? Natalie sat up straighter. Did she mean Daddy's care? While her sisters exchanged nervous glances, Natalie wrestled with her conflicting emotions. This would be the time to mention Charlotte and Forever Love. Yet she was torn. They would probably call her selfish. Maybe she was. But they weren't the ones who'd sacrificed their dreams to keep the farm going. Didn't she deserve an opportunity to chase her dreams, too? Certainly they'd warm to the idea when she told them Forever Love was offering $200,000?

She cleared her throat. "I—I have a suggestion. More of a proposal, really."

Everyone's heads swiveled her direction. Cami arched an eyebrow before taking another sip of her coffee.

"What if an unexpected opportunity came up?"

Natalie forced herself to meet her mother's confused gaze. "Daddy's long-term care will be very expensive, and we could—"

"We're not going to discuss long-term care right now." Mama glared at her. "Let's keep it positive, shall we?"

Natalie winced and shot Kirsten a pleading glance. *Help.*

Daddy cleared his throat. "I'm not interested in leaving my home."

Natalie sighed. "I didn't say you had to leave."

"I trust your judgment, and I'll listen to what you have to say, but I'm a long way from packing up and moving to an old folks' home."

Mama blanched and then lifted her cup to her lips and took a sip.

Natalie leaned back, the wicker pressing against her spine. Why wasn't Mama willing to say more? Surely she knew what was ahead. Did she really think they could handle Daddy's degenerative condition on their own? "I—I'm sorry. I didn't mean to be so insensitive. I just assumed you'd want to talk about your options before…" She trailed off. *Before things got really bad.*

"This affects all of us for different reasons." Daddy's brilliant blue eyes found hers. "My biggest issue with leaving is…what it represents. Everything you see here is part of our family's heritage. Seeing the farm, the kids visiting, people enjoying themselves—it keeps me going. Moving feels like giving up, and I—I'm just not ready to surrender."

Tears blurred her vision as his words sank in. When he put it like that, she *did* feel selfish. She didn't want him to give up, either. None of them wanted that. *This is horrible.* She could run a farm and appease a dozen high-maintenance brides, but she was ill-prepared to handle a disease that would rob Daddy of his faculties.

Cami passed her a napkin and kept one for herself. Natalie dabbed at the corners of her eyes. He'd made his feelings clear. She couldn't bring up Forever Love now.

Tisha broke the silence. "If this is where you want to spend the rest of your life, then I think you should get to stay."

"I know you don't want to discuss it, Mama, but there's still the issue of long-term care and what that will look like. The fact is, patients with Lou Gehrig's need a great deal of assistance." Kirsten's teary gaze flitted around the circle. "You'll need a substantial amount of money, possibly twenty-four-hour care. Is this house ideal for that, or should you consider a home better suited to meet your needs?"

See? How could they argue with that?

Frustration and guilt simmered within. Asking her family to support her decision to sell meant she could leave knowing she'd made a significant contribution to her parents' long-term care. Except Daddy's declining condition indicated she wouldn't be around to enjoy the last of his "good" days, or walk with her family through the darkest days of living with Lou Gehrig's.

An icy ball of dread settled in her stomach. What kind of a daughter walked away in the face of such a grim prognosis?

Darkness had long since fallen outside the kitchen windows in the new house. Shay drummed his fingers on the granite countertop and stared at the neat stacks of ceramic tile in front of him. No patterns or fancy designs involved—how hard could it be?

He'd spent the last fifteen minutes scarfing down a cheeseburger and fries while trying to convince himself he could figure this out. A collection of drawer pulls and cabinet knobs, still wrapped in plastic, sat in a pile beside the sink. He could take the easy road and install all the hardware, leaving the backsplash for another team of volunteers. But what if no one else showed up tonight? They'd run out of time. Everything needed to be finished today.

The front door opened, and Natalie came in carrying a container he hoped was filled with something sweet to power him through this late-night project.

"Oh, wow." A smile stretched across her face. "The cabinets look amazing."

Shay surveyed the latest addition to the kitchen. "Do you like them?"

"Like them?" She closed the door, and then she crossed to the counter and ran one hand along the edge. "I love them. You have no idea how awesome this is. I didn't think this was actually going to happen."

"Trent said they pulled together and knocked it out."

"When did the guys leave?"

He shrugged. "They were gone when I got here a little while ago."

"That's too bad. I wanted to say thank you." She pulled the plastic lid from the container, revealing a batch of chocolate chip cookies. Perfect. His mouth watered as she set them next to the tile.

"Are those for backsplash installers or only cabinet guys?"

"I'm more than happy to share. It would be a shame to let them go to waste."

"It certainly would."

She gestured with a flourish of her hand. "Enjoy."

"Thank you." He selected one and took a bite. "Mmmm, these are good," he mumbled around a mouthful of moist, sugary cookie, mixed with chocolate chunks.

"Wish I could take credit, but Erin sent them over." She twisted her hair into a bun at the back of her head, making him forget the tedious assignment he'd committed to. This might be doable now that she'd arrived, smelling like fall and plying him with sweets. He polished off the cookie and then wiped the crumbs from his fingertips on his jeans.

"Have you ever installed tile before?" She slipped out of her fleece jacket and draped it over a step stool. Once again, she'd managed to look adorable in worn-out jeans and a sorority fund-raiser T-shirt. If this tile didn't end up crooked, he'd be surprised.

"Shay?" Natalie leaned on the edge of the counter. "Have you done subway tile like this?"

"Nope, not in a kitchen. Only my in-laws' bathroom." He reached for his tape measure, praying she didn't ask any more questions about Monica's folks. Maybe he shouldn't give her a chance. "I've got to be honest. This is a big job. I'm willing to give it a shot—"

"Oh, no. Don't say it."

He swung his gaze her direction. "Say what?"

She held a cookie halfway to her mouth. "I can hear the disclaimer coming. Tell me. Whatever it is, I can take it."

Stretching the metal tape out, he measured the sliver of wall between the base of the cabinets and the edge of the granite countertop. "I can't stay up all night to pull this off. If we can't get it done, do you have anyone else who can step in and finish tomorrow?"

A brief silence filled the air while she finished chewing. "How could you possibly work through the night? Is someone staying with the boys?"

"My mom." He let the tape snap back into its

canister. "She felt guilty when she heard I'd hired someone else to babysit, so she's staying with us while the nanny is home for fall break and my dad is out of town."

"You don't need to stay up all night installing tile. That's crazy."

"Aren't you going to give this family their keys tomorrow at the concert?"

"Yep. We've already invited them—can't change our minds now."

He found a pencil in his toolbox and scribbled the measurements on a scrap of paper. "Without the backsplash finished? Or drawer pulls installed?"

"I know it sounds impossible. There's a lot that still needs to be done. I get it. But if there's one thing I've learned through all of this, it's that incredible things happen when people pull together. Let's get started, anyway. If all the tools and supplies are here, we have to at least try, right?"

An innocent statement on her part. Yet it twisted him in knots. If that was her outlook, why didn't it apply to relationships, too? He gave her a long look, debating whether to engage in a difficult conversation.

Her eyes widened. "What?"

"Nothing." He shoved back those dangerous thoughts and turned away in favor of locating a small sheet of sandpaper. Where had he seen it last?

"You had a strange expression on your face. What were you going to say?"

Shay found the sandpaper under a discarded paper bag from the fast food restaurant and then pivoted around to face her. Good thing the counter provided a buffer between them. A dot of chocolate lingered at the corner of her mouth, and he longed to kiss it away. "You said if we have everything we need, we have to at least try. So, I'm mentally processing what happens if we leave things…unresolved. That's not exactly my thing."

"If we get it started and can't finish it all, then we—wait a second." She narrowed her gaze. "Are we still talking about tile?"

"Yep." He formed his lips into a smile while his pulse ratcheted up a notch. She was on to him. Dancing right up to the edge of this topic was a reckless decision. If he didn't steer the conversation in a different direction, he'd have to confront these complex emotions tumbling around inside. He wasn't ready. "Why? What did you think I was talking about?"

She regarded him for another long second. "I—I don't know. Maybe I'm extra sensitive these days. Never mind."

"That's understandable." He searched her face. "How are things with your family?"

She massaged her forehead with her fingertips. "Not great. We're all pretty overwhelmed by this diagnosis."

"I'm sorry you're going through this."

"Thanks." She offered a tired smile. "We should probably get to work."

"Here." He held out a trowel and sandpaper. "Would you rather spread adhesive on the wall or sand the back of the tiles?"

She took the sandpaper from him. "I'll sand the tiles, I guess."

"Sounds good. I'll get started then." Turning away, he grabbed the adhesive and opened the lid, trying to focus on the project before him. His unmistakable feelings of attraction toward her battled against his cautious, practical nature. What if he was being too cautious, though? Hadn't he decided he was tired of playing it safe? He couldn't let his fears about past hurts keep getting in the way of his future. He'd finally admitted to himself he wanted to be much more than friends. But she'd also been authentic about her own loss. His heart fisted in his chest. Would she be able to love another firefighter?

The next evening, Natalie stood at the back of the high school auditorium, her cowboy boots tapping to the beat of Jayce Philips's latest hit, which was blasting from the speakers. He worked the edge of the stage as he sang the familiar lyrics and shook hands with the squealing girls in the front row of the packed house.

Caroline and Trent stood to her left, swaying to the music. Natalie looked past them, scanning the faces nearby for Shay. They'd finished the tile backsplash in the wee hours of the morning. She wouldn't blame him if he stayed home tonight. But part of her hoped he'd still show up for a little while, at least for the presentation of the house keys after Jayce's performance. After all he'd invested in the project, it would be so rewarding to meet the veteran and his family and see them accept the keys to their new home.

A jab in her upper arm captured her attention.

"What?" Natalie glanced at Caroline, who tilted her head toward the double doors. Butterflies pummeled Natalie's ribcage as Shay weaved his way through the crowd, an easy smile meant only for her spreading across his face. He wore a brown leather jacket and trendy dark-washed jeans—quite a nice change from his firefighter's uniform or old work clothes he wore at the building site. Most of his coworkers lined the back wall next to Trent, and Shay worked his way down, slapping shoulders and exchanging fist bumps.

Natalie worked moisture into her mouth as he stopped next to her and gave her arm a gentle squeeze. He leaned close to her ear. "Hey. You look pretty tonight."

His breath, warm against her cheek, pebbled her flesh with goose bumps. She smiled up at him. "Thank you."

The now-familiar fragrance of his woodsy aftershave lingered in the air as he settled against the wall beside her. She longed to tuck her hand in the crook of his elbow or lace her fingers through his. After their cryptic conversation last night over tile and chocolate chip cookies, it seemed too bold a move. Especially with the whole town looking on, including most of the guys from the fire department. She'd have to be content with his shoulder brushing against hers and bask in the glow of that heart-stopping grin of his.

Jayce ended the song, and a roar of approval rippled through the audience. "Thank you very much." He stood in the spotlight at center stage, a broad smile evident behind the microphone. "I'm thrilled to be here tonight. Thank you for inviting me. There's nothing better than performing in your hometown. It's a dream come true for me to be up here on this stage."

More cheers and applause ensued. Natalie clapped, too, grateful the details had come together for Jayce to be a part of the festival this year.

He raised his voice to be heard. "Speaking of dreams coming true, I've brought a special guest along—someone who also grew up dreaming about doing this country music thing. Her new album just dropped, and I know you've heard her first single on the radio, because everybody's playing it. Please give a warm Meadow Springs welcome for my friend Monica Ramsey!" Jayce stepped back, motioning for someone to join him.

"Oh, wow," Natalie murmured as a petite blond walked on stage wearing skintight jeans with several strategically placed rips on each leg, black ankle boots and a lacy black top layered over a camisole. Even from the back of the auditorium, her appearance was stunning.

"Thank you so much, Jayce," Monica said as the band launched into the first notes of "You Don't Know Me." Jayce wasn't kidding. The local country station played this one at least three times a day.

Shay pushed through the crowd and disappeared through the double doors.

Caroline and Natalie exchanged worried glances.

Natalie leaned across Caroline and spoke to Trent. "Do you know what that's about?"

He shook his head. "Not a clue."

She straightened, their conversation about tastes in music coming to mind. Shay had made his opinions about the country genre very clear. But that hardly seemed like a reason to rush out of the concert. Maybe he needed to make a phone call or decided to check on the boys. He'd let her know if there was an emergency, right?

Monica belted out the chorus, and Natalie tried to sing along. Shay's unexpected departure left a pit in her stomach, though, and the words died on her lips. This didn't feel normal.

"I'm going after him." She almost had to yell for Caroline to hear her.

Caroline nodded and patted her arm.

Shouldering her purse, Natalie squeezed through the crowd. All the guys from the station watched her go. This would probably be the highlight of their next meal together. She didn't care. Finding Shay was all that mattered.

Pushing through the doors, Natalie jogged across the empty foyer, her boots clicking on the checkered linoleum. A blast of cold air hit her as she moved outside into the crisp, clear November evening. She scanned the parking lot. Cars occupied every possible space, making it difficult to see which direction he'd gone. Then she discovered a lone figure on a bench next to a sculpture in the common area. The familiar slope of the shoulders as he hunched forward, elbows propped on his knees, confirmed it was Shay.

She approached slowly, the lights from the parking lot casting a blue-gray hue across her path. "Shay? Are you all right?"

He stared up at her, eyes dark and his chest heaving. "Did you know she was performing tonight?"

"Who? Monica Ramsey?" She shook her head. "No, that was all Jayce's doing."

A muscle in Shay's jaw knotted tight. "He didn't ask permission to bring her on stage?"

"He's a headlining tour with a sold-out show in Raleigh tomorrow. His performance tonight is a huge favor to all of us, but he never mentioned bringing anyone else along." She sank down on the bench next to him, clutching her purse in her lap. "What's going on? Why are you upset?"

His hands balled in tight fists, Shay stared out across the parking lot. "Monica Ramsey is my ex-wife."

Chapter Twelve

"You're kidding." Natalie's voice was barely audible.

"I wish." Shay pushed to his feet, adrenaline still coursing through his veins. "Just like I wish the last eighteen months was all a bad dream."

"Jayce never mentioned he was going to do this. Honest. If I'd known you'd see your ex-wife on stage tonight, I'd have given you plenty of advance notice."

Staring at the harvest moon hanging yellow-gold in the night sky, he measured his words carefully. This isn't how he imagined this conversation going down. There was so much he needed to share—wanted to share. But not like this. "I never told you her name, so how could you have known?"

"As the committee chairperson, I—I feel partly responsible. Is there anything I can do?"

Stay. The word flashed through his head like a bolt of lightning. It was a bold request—one he knew she couldn't accommodate. She probably had a dozen things to oversee before the night ended.

Brushing back his doubt, he pivoted to face her. "Could you sit with me? Or do you have to go back inside?"

She pulled her phone from her bag and checked the screen. "No. The presentation of the keys isn't until intermission. I've got a little while."

He settled onto the bench again and leaned forward, curling his fingers around the wooden seat. "I'm still…reeling. Part of me figured we'd see each other again someday. Then the months went by, and I never heard a word. The boys and I got used to doing life without her. But seeing her on stage—it feels like someone poured salt in an open wound. I had to get out of there."

"Did you know she was singing professionally?"

"I knew her album was out, but I avoided stations that played her music."

"I noticed."

"I still can't wrap my mind around it. She leaves her husband, her family. Never looks back. Yet a record deal and touring with a hot new star falls right in her lap." He shook his head. "Unbelievable."

"Has singing always been a part of her life?"

"Oh, yeah. Monica made it very clear from day one how much singing meant to her. We started dating our sophomore year in college, and by our senior year, she was singing two nights a week wherever she could. Then I proposed after graduation, and we got married the following Christmas. She begged me to move to Nashville, but I'd already started my first job at a fire station in Virginia, and I didn't want to start over again." He squeezed his eyes shut at the memory of their more heated arguments—painful accusations hurled like firecrackers. When she started sleeping at her best friend's house the nights he was on shift, he'd dismissed it as typical behavior for a newlywed firefighter's wife. Looking back, he recognized it as a symptom of a much larger problem.

"We struggled from the very beginning—petty disagreements, frustrated about each other's career ambitions. Then the boys came along, and she seemed content. Or maybe that's what I fooled myself into believing. Shortly after they turned six months old, she left. Said she couldn't put her dreams on hold any longer."

Natalie pressed her fingers against the sleeve of his jacket. "I'm sorry she's here, stirring up past hurts."

"Me, too." He stole another quick glance at the closed doors of the auditorium. What would happen if he and Monica crossed paths here in Meadow Springs?

"Do you think—would you want to speak with—"

"No." His whole body stiffened. "There's no way. I've got nothing left to say to her."

"Okay." Natalie inched away, withdrawing her hand. "It was just an idea."

"Unless her parents told her, she wouldn't even know the boys and I live here. Once she signed the papers, she relinquished all visitation rights. Deserted her own babies. She was so myopic—so focused on getting what she wanted."

"I can imagine it might be very confusing for the boys to see her."

"She's been gone for more than half their lives. How could any good come from it?" His heart ached for Liam and Aiden. They didn't deserve this. He'd do anything to protect them from more hurt.

"I'm sure this level of rejection is difficult to move past. Anyone in your position would be upset seeing their former spouse unexpectedly. Please don't let one woman's poor choices ruin your opinion of all of us, all right?"

He heard the gentle smile in her voice. "Ironic advice, coming from a wedding planner. You're probably required to give me a pep talk on romance."

"It sounds cheesy, I know. Still, I refuse to allow past experiences to sour my belief in lasting love. When I see my parents' commitment to one another, or watch countless couples begin their married life together... No matter what's happened before, I guess I'm still one of those crazy idealists that thinks happily-ever-after isn't just a fairy tale."

"I'm glad you still cling to that hope."

"Does that mean you don't?"

"No. I mean, yes. I—I still have hope. Liam and Aiden shouldn't have to grow up without a mother. I don't want to be a single dad forever." Shay raked a hand through his hair. Was he even making sense? Monica's reappearance dredged up all kinds of emotions. He couldn't think straight. Natalie was great with the boys. They were certainly crazy about her. She'd blown right past his defenses and taken up residence in his heart.

"They're sweet little boys and deserve a stepmother who will love them like her own." A muffled alarm rang from inside Natalie's purse. "That's my reminder. Ten minutes until intermission."

"Hang on. I— That sounded like—" He sighed, irritated with himself for tripping over his words. He couldn't let her go without acting on these feelings he'd tried half-heartedly to staunch.

A text message alert chimed on his phone. He pulled it from his pocket and glanced at the screen. Mom. Could her timing be any worse?

Sorry to spoil your fun. Boys are vomiting. Please come home.

"Great," Shay muttered. "The boys are sick."

"Ugh. I'm sorry." She pushed to her feet. "They're expecting me inside for the presentation, so I should go."

His pulse kicked into overdrive. *Say something.* He stood, determined to redeem what was left of the evening—determined to tell her he wanted her in his life.

"Natalie, wait."

She hesitated, her purse dangling from one hand.

"Thank you for coming after me." He reached out and caressed her arm. "It means a lot."

"You're welcome." Her stunning blue eyes stayed riveted on his. "I wish I could do more to help."

"Are you kidding? I think you're amazing. My boys are crazy about you, too. You're different than any woman I've ever known—you have such a huge heart, always putting the needs of the people you love and care about first. I really like you, Natalie. I—I know we said we'd just be friends, but I'm hoping we can be more." He leaned in and brushed his lips against hers. She kissed him back, her palm pressed against his chest.

He slid his hands around her waist, gently pulling her closer, lost in the sensation of her touch, her sweet perfume enveloping him.

They both pulled back, and her mouth curved into a smile. "I'm sorry. I have to go." She let her fingertips trail down his jacket sleeves and then skim across his hand, lingering for a long moment before finally stepping away.

"Me, too. I hate that the boys are sick." His arms ached to reach for her and kiss her again.

"I hope they feel better soon." She waved and then pivoted and jogged toward the auditorium.

He stared after her, a smile still playing on his lips. Maybe, just maybe, this was the beginning of something wonderful.

Natalie waited backstage in the auditorium, the taste of Shay's kiss still on her lips and his words echoing in her head.

I think you're amazing.

The floorboards beneath her boots vibrated from the drums as Jayce and Monica sang a duet before the intermission. Peeking inside the envelope in her hand, she confirmed the new house keys were still there. *You've got this.* As much as she wanted to dwell on the details of Shay's tender kiss and his kind words, it was time to focus. Tonight was all about making one deserving family's dream come true.

Monica Ramsey strode past her, chest heaving, as she handed her microphone to a volunteer nearby. Natalie stepped back, trying to blend into the thick, dark curtains marking the edge of the stage. A middle-aged man wearing black from head to toe offered Monica a bottle of water and then whispered in her ear. She smiled before twisting off the cap and taking a long sip. The wide neckline of her shirt slipped off her shoulder, revealing the thin black strap of her camisole and a butterfly tattoo.

Hateful thoughts forced their way into Natalie's

head. How she longed to march over, armed with adorable photos of Aiden and Liam on her phone to wave in the starlet's flawless face. Hit song or not, didn't she know what she was missing?

Monica glanced over, and Natalie averted her gaze to the notes she'd scribbled on the back of the envelope. It wasn't her place to say anything to Shay's ex-wife. Her visceral reaction to Monica's presence surprised her, though. She knew it meant she genuinely cared about Shay and the boys—as more than friends. That kiss outside proved they both wanted more.

Her heart fisted in her chest. The full impact of her decision about Forever Love weighed heavily. She'd submitted her counteroffer this morning. Would Charlotte be worth it?

Jayce's rich baritone summoned her. She filled her lungs with a ragged breath, praying for the strength to get through this announcement and safely off stage without any hiccups. There'd be plenty of time to second-guess her choices later. The bright lights blinded her, but she pasted on a smile and headed straight for Jayce in the middle of the stage, just like they'd rehearsed.

"Miss Natalie, come over here with me." Jayce waved her closer, like they were old friends instead of acquaintances who happened to be from the same small town.

Her pulse thrumming in her chest, Natalie halted

her steps next to Jayce and clutched the envelope tighter to keep her hands from shaking.

"I understand you have a big announcement for some special guests in our audience?" A broad smile stretched across Jayce's boyish face as he offered her the microphone.

"That's correct, Jayce." Natalie angled toward the crowd. "As many of you know, a huge team of volunteers have worked tirelessly to build a house that's move-in ready before the holidays. I'd like to thank everyone for their generous contributions— whether it was your time, financial support, building supplies—none of this would've been possible without all of you pitching in. Thank you, Meadow Springs. You're the best."

She paused while another wave of applause swept through the room.

"As I've traveled the country, I tell everybody how proud I am to be from Meadow Springs, North Carolina. This is such an amazing community," Jayce rumbled into the microphone. "Tell us more about this awesome house and the family that gets to move in soon."

"I'd love to." Natalie took the microphone again and scanned her notes quickly. Then she glanced at the honored guests seated in the front row. "Captain Wilson completed multiple tours of duty in Iraq and Afghanistan, where he was awarded the Silver Star for his heroic efforts in combat. A graduate of NC State and a devoted hockey fan, Ben and his wife, Samantha, have a four-year-old daughter, and they're expecting a second child any day now. Please give a warm welcome to Ben, Samantha and Sadie Wilson."

Hot tears pricked Natalie's eyes as the crowd rose to their feet and gave a standing ovation. She was so proud of her hometown and the way they'd risen to the occasion to help this family. Jayce was right. This was a phenomenal community.

After she presented the keys to Captain Wilson and his family, Natalie followed Jayce off stage, where a small contingent from the local media waited for a photo op. She had zero interest in posing for a picture. Quickening her pace, she slipped out the side door and back into the crisp evening air.

The lights from the football field cast a blue-gray glow over the grassy area beside the school. Families with young children lined the sidewalk, eagerly awaiting their turn to play the ring toss game or throw darts at balloons, determined to win one of the coveted prizes. She caught a glimpse of two little blond boys in the crowd and the hollow ache of disappointment filled her chest. Too bad Aiden and Liam weren't feeling well. She'd hoped to enjoy the festival with them. Shay, too. She could stay and mingle on her own, right? Savor every minute of one of her favorite things about this place she'd called home for almost thirty years. If Forever Love accepted her counteroffer, tonight might be her last festival in Meadow Springs.

Chapter Thirteen

Shay slid the last of the breakfast plates into the dishwasher and tucked a detergent capsule in the slot on the door. Straightening, he surveyed the counter one last time for any leftover utensils or glasses. He couldn't wait to knock out the last of his chores, line up for roll call and then head home to see Aiden and Liam.

They seemed to have recovered from the vomiting virus. Maybe he'd rake a giant pile of leaves in the yard and show them how to jump in it. Or if they were up for an adventure, he could brave one of the nearby state parks and throw rocks in the creek. Although more than likely, they'd both campaign for another visit to the farm. He smiled. Not that he could blame them. He was eager to see Natalie again. The last three days since the concert felt more like three years.

Closing the door on the dishwasher, he turned it

on and pivoted away from the counter, only to find Chief Murphy blocking his path.

Shay flinched. "Sorry, sir. I didn't hear you come in."

"No problem. I wanted to catch you before everybody lined up for roll call."

"Oh? What's going on?"

"I'm checking in, that's all." The chief's penetrating gaze made Shay squirm. Had he overlooked a piece of equipment? Made the coffee too strong? Gone to bed without shutting off all the lights in the station? None of those tiny infractions seemed worthy of a private conversation.

"I—I'm not sure I follow."

"How are things at home?"

Shay rocked back on his heels. "Mostly fine, as far as I know. Why?"

"I've never been in your situation." Murphy scrubbed his fingertips along his jaw. "Single parenthood must be tough, especially with two little kids and an unusual work schedule. You seem to be settling into a routine, and yesterday I noticed an extra spring in your step." His expression softened. "I like you, Campbell. You're an excellent firefighter and an asset to this station. I want to make sure things are going as well as can be expected."

"This move was a big adjustment—much harder than I anticipated—but you're right. We're settling into a good routine." Shay looked down, rubbing the back of his neck with his palm. He hadn't seen Natalie since they kissed outside the auditorium, so they hadn't had a chance to talk about their relationship status. It wasn't something he cared to mention to his boss, even if she was part of the reason for his positive attitude. "With a little more time, I think things will only continue to improve."

"That's good to hear." Chief Murphy pulled out one of the kitchen chairs and gestured for Shay to do the same. "There's no need to worry. Your probationary status isn't in jeopardy. I'm letting you know that I've sensed a more optimistic vibe, and I think it's a good thing."

The tension in Shay's body loosened a little, and he sat in a seat opposite Chief Murphy. "Childcare will probably be an ongoing issue for me, to be perfectly honest. My mother looks after the boys when I'm working. Lately my father has expressed some frustration with our arrangement, so I hired a nanny. It's working out okay, but I'm not crazy about it, and financially, it's a...challenge."

"I see. Are you uncomfortable leaving the boys alone with the nanny?"

"No. Of course not. I mean, Aiden has a life-threatening peanut allergy, but she's very cautious, and so far, it hasn't been a problem. It's still hard on the boys, especially when they've already experienced a lot of upheaval." Shay cringed, recalling the epic tantrum Liam threw when he left for his shift. It was all he could do to get in the truck and drive to work without having a meltdown of his own.

The kitchen chair creaked as Murphy leaned back. "Would you feel more at ease if your parents agreed to provide consistent care?"

"Absolutely. But I don't see that happening." After the play structure debacle, he and his father had barely spoken. As far as he knew, his parents hadn't altered their vacation plans, either, which meant he desperately needed to find childcare before his next shift.

"I'm happy to work something out if you need to adjust your schedule. I can approve additional shift trades or—"

"That won't be necessary, sir. I'll figure this out." He hoped his tone masked his underlying worry. Boarding school had taught him to be self-sufficient. Even though his faith was important to him, hadn't the last two years demonstrated that Aiden and Liam's security was ultimately up to him? So why the constant struggle to keep his family afloat?

"I won't force your hand. That's not how I operate." Chief Murphy pushed back his chair and stood. "The offer for scheduling adjustments still stands. I hope you'll keep that in mind."

"Thank you. I appreciate it."

Shay followed him out to the garage, taking his place in line for roll call. As the new shift reported for duty, he greeted the guys and then headed for his truck at the earliest opportunity. Wispy clouds dotted the pale blue sky, hinting at another beautiful fall day. The chief's inquiry gnawed at him. Even though Murphy had asked about things at home with the best of intentions, Shay's performance was obviously being closely observed. Despite the offer for a schedule change, there's no way he'd ask for special accommodations or favors now.

Steering his truck out of the parking lot, Shay's thoughts circled back to his admission to Chief Murphy that childcare was a challenge. Maybe he should've kept that to himself. Everybody at the station probably had something going on at home they struggled with, but he was the only single parent. He didn't want to be the guy who needed favors all the time, especially when he was still on probation. Firefighting was a great career, and changing jobs didn't appeal to him, either. But paying the nanny for overnight stays was eating away at his savings, and if he couldn't provide for the boys, he'd be forced to rely on his parents for even more help. The very thought of asking his dad to bail him out left a bad taste in his mouth.

He slowed down at the entrance to the farm, his heart rate kicking up a notch at the thought of seeing Natalie. *Enough with the second-guessing.*

After parking, he sent a quick text to the nanny, letting her know he had to run a quick errand before he got home. Then he took a minute to gather his thoughts and pray. Asking Natalie for help felt like a big step, but a positive one. She'd already offered once, and the boys loved being around her. Now was the time to humbly invite her into his world and all the messiness it entailed.

Natalie stood alone inside Magnolia Lane, unpacking supplies for centerpieces from a rubber storage bin. The barn required a significant transformation for two upcoming weddings and several holiday parties. Deposits had been collected, and Bridget was scheduled to manage these events. The proverbial show had to go on. The least Natalie could do was get a head start on the preparations.

She glanced at the time on her phone and then let her eyes wander to her email. On the advice of a trusted friend who worked in commercial real estate, when she'd countered Forever Love's offer, she'd asked for a higher sale price, given the combined value of the land, venue and her future bookings. Since she'd felt uncertain about the events already scheduled being a part of the acquisition, her friend had crafted what he jokingly referred to as an escape clause, as well. Both parties had seven days after acceptance to back out.

Even though she'd vowed to quit stalking her inbox, Natalie had already checked her messages at least ten times today. Karen and Penny hadn't responded. Maybe they'd changed their minds. Her stomach clenched. What if the whole deal fell through? Then she'd never have to mention it to Shay. Since the boys had been sick, they hadn't had a chance to connect. But she hadn't stopped thinking about that incredible kiss, and she caught herself daydreaming more than once about a relationship with him.

She sighed and put her phone down. With only a few minutes until one of her December brides-to-be arrived for a consultation, she reached for another storage container to occupy her hands. And her thoughts.

Why was this so hard? Charlotte seemed almost within her grasp. The festival had gone off without a hitch, and the Wilson family moved into their brand-new home, just in time to welcome a healthy new baby girl. But Magnolia Lane's uncertain status prevented the last of the details from falling into place. Maybe it was for the best that Forever Love hadn't responded yet. She had no idea how she'd break the news to Shay that she'd sold her business and planned to move away.

The door opened, and Natalie turned around, expecting to see her client.

Shay filled the doorway, his surprise appearance—in uniform, no less—making her pulse bounce around like a pinball. She drew a deep breath and tried to act casual. "Oh. Hi."

"Is this a bad time?"

"No, of course not." Tempted to close the gap between them and plant a kiss on his cheek, she forced herself to keep some space, in case her client arrived. Besides, he looked nervous. "What's up?"

"How's the event planning business?"

She gave him a long look. Had he really dropped by to say hello? That was sweet of him, especially if he'd come from the station. "This is kind of the calm before the storm. Too close to Thanksgiving for wedding receptions, and too early for holiday parties."

Jamming his hands in his pockets, he worked his jaw back and forth. "Remember when we were painting that room and you offered to help watch the boys?"

"Uh-huh." It felt like a lifetime ago, rather than only a couple of weeks.

"Were you serious?"

"About watching the boys?" She set a spool of ribbon on the table. "Depends on when you need my help."

"Any chance you're available this weekend?"

Whoa. "The whole weekend?"

"I know it's short notice. I should've asked sooner. I'm sure you have plans."

"I'm not scheduled to work. Things are pretty quiet at the farm, too." Her weekend originally involved packing tape and cardboard boxes. Without an official acceptance of her counteroffer, that seemed premature.

"The nanny told me when she accepted the position that she had a wedding in Charleston this weekend. I wouldn't ask just anyone, you know."

He inched closer and gently clasped her upper arms with his hands. "You're special to us."

The warmth of his touch sent a delicious tingle zinging through her. "Thanks for that vote of confidence." She teased, tipping her chin up. "Are you sure you trust me with your children?"

Two spots of color clung to his cheekbones. "That's a fair question. Of course, I trust you. The boys like to be with you, and you've been great with them."

"What happens if I say no?"

Brow furrowed, he pulled back and shoved his hands in his pockets. "Then I'll be forced to ask Chief Murphy to find coverage for my shift, or else call in sick. Neither of which are wise choices."

"How will we handle the food allergy thing? Your expectations are…intense."

"I've written all of the instructions and expectations out. I'll email the document today if you'd like."

Despite her misgivings, she couldn't stop her smile from forming. "A written protocol. That's impressive."

He lifted his shoulders. "I try."

"Will Aiden and Liam feel comfortable with me? Two days is a long time."

"There will be some crying—okay, a lot of crying—when I leave. If you redirect or distract them, they usually calm down."

She examined her fingernails. Distract or redirect. Did that mean spending countless hours at the farm? That wasn't such a tough assignment. Rex and his team were in the midst of stringing all the lights for their Christmas extravaganza. She could probably convince him to take the boys for a tractor ride or two. But the significance of Shay's plea wasn't lost on her. Asking for her help was a big step. He was letting his guard down and allowing her into his life—embracing the possibility of a relationship.

Her mouth went dry. What was she going to do about Forever Love now? She'd made up her mind. Hadn't she?

Brushing aside the niggling questions, she conceded to help. "I'd be happy to take care of the boys this weekend."

Relief washed over his face. "Thank you so much. Seriously. You have no idea." He pulled her into a hug. Her heart thumped against her ribs as her arms responded, encircling Shay's back. *What just happened?* The words died on her tongue, and she closed her eyes, savoring the security of his embrace. It felt good to be held, with her head tucked under his chin, as if she belonged there. Maybe it was a blessing she hadn't heard from Penny or Karen yet. Maybe she'd need another day or two to rethink the Forever Love thing, after all.

"You're welcome," she finally mumbled against the rough fabric of his uniform, and then she quickly pulled away and reached for her phone on the table. "You have my phone number and email address, right?"

She could do this. "Aiden, let's put your jacket on. It's chilly outside."

"No, no, no." Aiden toddled across the living room, a toy car he'd insisted on holding all morning—so Liam couldn't—encased in his chubby fist.

"No, no." Liam parroted, chasing after him.

Natalie sighed. By the time she convinced them to put on their jackets and shoes, wrestled them into the double stroller and pushed them to the park, it would be time to turn around and come home for lunch. After spending the early morning hours cleaning up the aftermath of breakfast and refereeing their arguments, she'd abandoned her ambitious plans for a trip to the farm. The park felt equally as daunting, but she had to get them out of the house. Shay had told hcr at least twice that fresh air did wonderful things for little boys and ensured long afternoon naps. If there was one thing she coveted, it was a nap.

"Liam, if you put your jacket on, I'll give you a yummy treat." Shay would not be impressed that she'd resorted to bribery, but his instructions clearly stated that animal crackers were acceptable on rare occasions.

Liam whirled around, his smooth brow puckered. She pulled the red box from her bag and gently rattled the contents. Aiden dropped the car and raced to meet her.

"Eat? Eat?" He bounced up and down at her feet.

"As soon as you're dressed and sitting in the stroller, I'll let you have some."

"Me, me." Patting his chest, he scrambled to grab his shoes before Liam did.

Sensing he might be left out, Liam stood with his shoes dangling from each hand, tears welling in his eyes already.

"Okay, okay." She softened at his tenderhearted reaction. This was probably just as hard for them as it was for her. They were certainly adorable. Not to mention generous with their spontaneous cuddles. And Aiden's belly laugh made her smile every time. Despite her best efforts, they'd sent her heart careening off track, in the best kind of detour. Visions of caring for them on a more permanent basis played at the back of her mind. Maybe she could say no to Charlotte if it meant yes to a life with Shay and his boys.

Whoa. *Slow down.* It was a big leap from "more than friends" to happily-ever-after. Is that really what Shay wanted?

She tamped down her convoluted emotions and hurried to stuff little arms into sleeves and put shoes on feet, before her window of opportunity closed. "Thank you for listening, boys. Let's go find your stroller."

She ushered them outside and across the driveway to the detached garage. Huge maple leaves littered the driveway, capturing the boys' attention long enough for her to open the garage door with the PIN code Shay had provided. By the time she wheeled the stroller out and closed the door, they'd abandoned their new discovery.

"Eat?" Liam eyed the bag she'd slung over her shoulder.

"Get in, please." Natalie untangled the straps. "If you'll obey and let me buckle you in, I will give you the crackers."

They complied, even sitting still while she wrestled with securing the buckles over their bulky jackets.

"There." Natalie stepped back, perspiration collecting under her own fleece pullover. No time to celebrate her monumental achievement. She had to dispense the promised snack before mutiny broke out.

Opening the package, she gave them each two crackers, one for each hand. "Here you go."

The boys happily nibbled on their rewards, content to enjoy the ride, while she maneuvered the stroller down the driveway and onto the sidewalk. For all her determination to get Aiden and Liam outside, she hadn't given much thought to how quickly it might wear her out, too. A loaded stroller wasn't an easy thing to push. At least they didn't have far to go—the neighborhood park wasn't more than a block from the house.

Although she expected the playground to be empty, given the chilly bite in the air, another young woman sat huddled on a bench. Two little boys, not much older than Liam and Aiden, chased each other around the base of the red, blue and green play structure.

"Good morning." Natalie eased the stroller beside the bench, careful to set the brake before releasing the boys.

"Hey." The woman glanced up from her phone long enough to make eye contact and then went back to staring at the screen in her palm. Natalie chased away a twinge of envy. *Must be nice.* Maybe the boys would all play together, and she'd have a couple of minutes to scroll through her inbox or check for voice mail messages. Surely Forever Love would respond soon. Her counteroffer was reasonable, given the value of the land and recent comparable sales. And including an option to renege protected both parties, didn't it? She sighed. The waiting was about to drive her crazy.

Aiden and Liam headed straight for the sandbox, where plastic dump trucks, shovels and buckets were strewn about. Natalie opened her mouth to remind them to ask before they played with someone else's toys, but changed her mind when the other boys didn't object. Grateful for a few minutes of peace, she collapsed on the bench.

"Don't you wish you had half their energy?" The

woman put her phone away. "Mine could power a small country."

Natalie chuckled. "So true."

"How old are your boys?"

"Oh, they aren't mine. I'm babysitting for a friend. Aiden and Liam are two."

"Wow, you're a generous friend." She held out her hand. "I'm Kelly, by the way."

"Nice to meet you." She shook her hand. "Natalie McDowell. I—" The familiar ringtone of her phone sang from the side pocket of her bag.

"Go ahead. I'll keep an eye on them for you."

Natalie glanced at the sandbox. The boys seemed occupied. "Let me see who it is." She snagged the phone and checked the caller ID. A number with a Charlotte area code filled the screen. "Excuse me for one second."

Swiping her finger across the screen, she pressed the phone to her ear and said hello.

"Natalie? It's Karen, with Forever Love. How are you?"

Her heart rate sped up. "Hi, Karen. I'm well, thank you."

"Excellent. I have wonderful news. Is this a good time to chat?"

Natalie turned her back on the boys so she could concentrate. A short phone call couldn't hurt. It wasn't like she'd abandoned her post. Kelly said she'd watch them. Besides, this was important. "Now is fine."

"Penny and I have talked, and we accept your counteroffer. Isn't that wonderful?"

Natalie swallowed hard. Why didn't she share Karen's enthusiasm? "Wow. Yeah. I— That's great."

"We're thrilled to have you and can't wait to welcome you in person. We've signed the documents, and I'll email them to you today. All you have to do is sign and send them back. As you know, both parties have seven days to renege." She chuckled. "It sounds like we don't need to worry about that, though."

"Perfect."

"Thanks, Natalie. We'll chat again soon."

"Take care." She ended the call and then stared across the playground. This wasn't perfect at all. What about Shay? And the boys? The thought of leaving them now delivered a sucker punch to her soul.

Natalie trudged back toward the sandbox, fighting to keep her emotions in check.

Kelly smiled at her. "Good news?"

"Sort of. I've been waiting forever for this job offer, and they finally called."

"Awesome. Congratulations." She crumpled a plastic wrapper in her hand. "I gave the boys a granola bar. I hope that's okay. It's organic, high in protein, low in sugar, no fructose corn syrup. You know, all that stuff we ate growing up but wouldn't dream of feeding to our kids."

"Oh, no." Natalie's gaze flew to Aiden and then Liam, her heart in her throat. Their mouths were ringed with crumbs, and Aiden had chocolate smeared on his chin. "It didn't contain peanuts, did it?"

Kelly's face paled. "They have a peanut allergy?"

"Aiden does. It's severe."

"I'm so sorry." She cupped her hand to her mouth, panic in her eyes.

Natalie knelt beside Aiden and grasped his shoulders. He held a dump truck in his lap, but rubbed his fingers over his lips. "Ouch."

"Ouch? Does your mouth hurt? Let me see." Natalie leaned closer. Were his lips swelling?

"What can I do? Tell me." Kelly dropped to her knees beside Natalie, grains of sand spraying onto their jeans.

Her mind raced. Shay had reviewed the signs and symptoms of an allergic reaction before he left. She was supposed to watch for swelling and an obstructed airway. Hives had formed on Aiden's cheek, and his nose was running. But he wasn't struggling to breathe. So maybe they were okay.

"Do you want me to call 911?" Kelly whipped out her phone.

Natalie hesitated. "Let's get his EpiPen first. If we have to use it, they'll need to talk me through the steps."

"Is it in your diaper bag?"

"Yes."

While Kelly ran and grabbed the bag from the stroller, Natalie pulled Aiden into her lap. He let go of the truck without a fight. And what was that sound? Like air being sucked through a—

"No," she whispered. "Aiden, does your chest hurt?"

He didn't answer, only dragged his sandy fingers across his mouth. She pressed her ear closer. The wheezing grew louder, making her stomach churn. *Please, Lord, don't let me lose him.*

"Kelly!" she screamed. "Call 911. He can't breathe."

Chapter Fourteen

Shay sat in the passenger seat of Chief Murphy's truck, a box of leaf collection bags at his feet. A slow morning at the fire station translated to yard work for the guys on duty. The chief had appointed Shay his wing man for a quick trip to the hardware store. Although Shay campaigned for taking the long way back to the station and grabbing donuts at Coffee at the Corner, Murphy had shot him down. "Too many leaves on the lawn," he'd grumbled.

Shay wanted to point out the project would probably move faster if donuts were involved, but thought better of it.

"Attention, Meadow Springs station twenty-first responders, allergic reaction, Park View Lane." The dispatcher's voice crackled through the speaker mounted inside the chief's truck. "Caller reports a Caucasian male, two years of age, experiencing possible anaphylactic shock after exposure to peanut allergen."

A shiver raked Shay's spine. Park View Lane. That was only one street over from his. "Aiden," he whispered, clawing at the truck's door handle.

Chief Murphy's thick fingers encircled Shay's arm in a vise grip. "Wait a second. You don't know if—"

"Stop the truck." Shay wrenched his arm free. "I've got to get over there."

Murphy slowed to a stop in the middle of Main Street. "Shay, listen to me. We're closer to the hospital than the park. If you're worried that's your son, I'll drive you over to the ER. We'll meet them there."

His heart hammered. "Take me to the park," he said through clenched teeth. What was Chief Murphy thinking?

"You're no help to him or our department if you respond to the call. Trust me. Does he carry an EpiPen?"

Shay slouched forward, squeezing his eyes shut. This couldn't be happening. "Yes. I mean, he's supposed to. Natalie McDowell's watching the boys…" He trailed off. What if she'd forgotten? He'd gone over all the instructions several times, but Aiden and Liam demanded so much physical energy, it was easy to forget important details. Especially if someone wasn't used to taking care of little kids.

"Rescue twenty en route." Hamilton's familiar

voice broke through his muddled thoughts. Shay's eyes popped open, and he stared at the radio, willing him to offer more—anything to ease his frantic worry. When no other details were given, he fumbled for his phone and scrolled quickly to Natalie's number. Jabbing at the screen, his body trembled as he held his breath and listened to it ring. Then ring some more. *C'mon, c'mon. Pick up.*

"Hey, this is Natalie. I'm sorry I missed your call. Please—"

Shay hung up and dropped his phone in his lap. "She didn't answer." He drummed his fist against the door while his mind raced.

Chief Murphy activated his siren and sped up, blowing through the traffic light overhead as it transitioned from green to yellow. "Since they've already responded, let's get you to the ER."

"Sir, I really need to get to the park. What about my other son? He'll be terrified if he's separated from Aiden." Shay squirmed in his seat, feeling trapped like a caged animal. Didn't Murphy get it? These were his *sons*. Possibly involved in a life-threatening emergency. It wasn't about being a good EMT or even a competent firefighter. He needed to be on the scene because these children were his life. His everything. All he had.

The chief shot him a quizzical look. "I can't tell you the number of times I've seen a firefighter respond to a family member in distress and come unglued. Do you want to risk compromising your child's care because they've got to restrain you, too?"

He snorted. "No one's going to have to restrain me."

"You'd be surprised what people do when their loved one is involved."

He couldn't argue with that. Fragments of the horrible day that forever changed him flashed in his memory. The kids in bathing suits lining the sandy strip, staring in horror. White-hot terror streaking through his little body as he slogged through the water, his feet squishing in the goopy mud coating the bottom of the pond. He'd never heard his mother scream like that before. Or since.

"Rescue twenty en route to Meadow Springs Community Hospital," the dispatcher said. "ETA four minutes."

"That's it?" He could no longer keep the desperation from his voice. "All we get is an estimated time of arrival?" He had to know more. Was Aiden in stable condition? Had they opened his airway? What about Liam? The questions piled up faster than he could form them into words. Straining against his safety belt, he craned his neck, searching for the hospital through the windshield.

"Food allergies are more common these days. It's entirely possible this isn't your son," Murphy reminded him. "We'll know more as soon as we get there. Anaphylactic shock is treatable with an injection, remember. The trip to the ER is for further evaluation and follow-up care."

"*If* he got the injection in time."

"They wouldn't hold off on the injection."

More sirens filled the air, and Murphy pulled over to allow the ambulance to pass him. Shay's stomach churned as the vehicle flew by in a blur, its blue lights flashing. *My boy is in there. Dear God, please protect him.*

"We're almost there." Murphy checked his mirrors before easing the truck back onto the two-lane street. Thankfully the small amount of Saturday morning traffic wasn't a hindrance.

The last two blocks felt like twenty. Shay dug his fingernails into the seat's upholstery until his knuckles turned white. *Hang on, Aiden. Daddy's coming.*

At last, the entrance to the hospital appeared on their right, and Murphy careened into the parking lot, siren still wailing. Bright red letters on a white sign directed them toward the emergency room. Three men and women dressed in green scrubs swarmed around the ambulance's double doors. Murphy steered the truck into the closest space and Shay unbuckled and jumped out before the wheels stopped rolling.

He sprinted across the asphalt. "Hey! That's my son."

Paul, one of the EMTs, whirled around, blocking Shay's path. "Shay, I'm going to have to ask you to stay back."

"You're out of your mind." Shay had at least twenty pounds and five inches on the guy. Brushing past him, he shoved his way into the huddle forming around the gurney. Aiden's little body was strapped to the white mattress, an oxygen mask covering his nose and mouth while he squinted against the brightness of the sunlight. Shay's throat constricted.

"Da-da!" Liam squealed from inside the ambulance.

Bryce, the EMT sitting with Liam, recognized Shay. "Are these your boys?"

Liam squirmed out of Bryce's grasp and toddled to the doorway, his eyes wide. Bryce steadied him before Liam could launch himself at Shay. "Hang on a sec, pal."

"Yes, these are my boys." Wasn't it obvious? Shay scanned the faces surrounding him, trying to identify the person in charge. "What happened?"

Aiden stretched an arm out, his words muffled by the heavy plastic mask.

Shay lunged and grasped Aiden's little hand in his. "I'm here, buddy. The doctors are going to take good care of you."

Aiden shook his head, tears slipping from the corner of his eye. Shay bit the inside of his cheek to keep his own emotions in check.

"Sir, I'm Doctor Wagner, the attending physician." A balding man wearing a white jacket over his scrubs stood on the other side of Aiden's gurney. "Your son was experiencing difficulty breathing secondary to something he'd ingested. His airway is open, and he's in stable condition. Why don't we move inside for further evaluation? You're more than welcome to bring your other child with you."

Shay nodded. "C'mon, Liam. Let's go with Aiden." He scooped Liam up, savoring the comfort of his child's arms flung around his neck. Resting his cheek against Liam's hair, he breathed in the familiar scent of baby shampoo. Whispering a prayer of thanks that both boys seemed to be okay, Shay carried Liam through the automatic doors and into the emergency room. As they moved through the waiting room, he realized no one had mentioned Natalie, and he hadn't seen her yet. Anger boiled up like molten lava. That was probably a blessing in disguise. He couldn't be responsible for what he might say or do when their paths crossed.

Natalie paced from one side of the hospital waiting room to the other, arms linked across her chest. Sand clung to the sleeves of her fleece pullover, but she didn't care. All she wanted was an update on Aiden.

Hours had passed since the EMTs had responded to her call for help, securing his tiny body on that giant gurney while she'd held a distraught Liam in her arms. One of the EMTs had taken Liam from her, too. Not that she blamed him. Obviously she couldn't be trusted. No matter how many times she asked the nurse at the desk for an update, the woman stubbornly refused to provide any details. Something about health information privacy. Whatever. She wasn't leaving until she knew for sure Aiden was okay.

"Can I get you anything? A bottle of water? Maybe a snack from the vending machine?" Erin's worried gaze followed her. "You'll feel better if you eat something."

Natalie shook her head and kept pacing. That wasn't true. She couldn't eat, anyway. Her stomach was twisted in knots. What if he didn't recover from her careless mistake? What if—

The doors to the restricted area opened with a *whoosh*, and Natalie spun around, hoping to see Shay. Nope. Only a nurse pushing an elderly gentleman in a wheelchair.

"Why can't anybody tell us something? This is ridiculous." Perching on the edge of a plastic chair, she fired another angry glance at the nurse behind the glass partition.

"I've texted Caroline. Maybe she's heard from Trent." Erin held her phone in her lap. "I'm sure she'll answer soon."

"I tried texting Shay. And calling. His phone goes straight to voice mail." The sick feeling in the pit of Natalie's stomach worsened with each passing minute. He was probably way too upset to speak with her.

"I'm sure we'll hear something soon." Erin crossed one leg over the other, her foot jiggling incessantly.

"He has to be all right. I mean, he was breathing when they put him in the ambulance. I find it hard to believe he—" Natalie couldn't bring herself to finish the sentence.

"If you don't mind my asking, what happened? Did he get into something when you weren't looking?"

Natalie scuffed the toe of her sneaker against the speckled linoleum. "I answered my phone."

"That's not a big deal. I see parents on their phones all the time when they're with their kids. You didn't leave the park, right?"

"No. I let a complete stranger watch the boys." She dropped her chin to her chest. If she could rewind the day's events, she never would've answered that call.

"Oh, Natalie." Erin reached over and squeezed her shoulder. "Is that who gave him the peanut butter?"

The doors opened again, and Natalie straightened. Instead of a familiar face, a doctor emerged and called someone's name.

Natalie slumped back in her chair. "It wasn't even peanut butter. She let him have a granola bar. I guess it had peanut residue on it."

"I thank the Lord you had the EpiPen with you."

Natalie nodded in agreement, while inwardly cringing at her lack of faith. Sure, she'd cried out for help in desperation an awful lot lately, but that wasn't the kind of shallow relationship with the Lord she truly wanted.

More guilt coiled her insides in tighter knots. Her biggest fear had come true—she'd become so focused on getting what she thought she'd wanted. Now someone she cared about—an innocent little boy who depended on her—had been hurt.

Please help me make this right, Lord, she pleaded silently, trembling as she imagined the worst possible outcome.

"So who were you talking to?" Erin leaned forward and rearranged the stack of worn magazines on the table.

Natalie flinched. Had she spoken her prayer out loud? "What?"

"The phone call you answered. Who was it?"

Picking at a hangnail on her thumb, Natalie braced for Erin's reaction. She hadn't meant to keep her plans a secret. At least not for this long. Between their jobs and the festival, they hadn't had a chance to talk—really talk—about anything.

"This is about the Charlotte thing, isn't it?"

She stared in disbelief. "How did you know?"

"Cami came in for coffee and asked me if I knew what was going on."

Natalie looked away so she wouldn't have to see the hurt in Erin's eyes.

"When were you planning to tell me?"

Massaging her forehead with her fingertips, Natalie struggled to map out a timeline. "This week, I guess."

"Right about the time you need me to come over and help pack?"

Ouch. "I didn't mean to wait this long."

"This better be the most incredible job opportunity ever."

She couldn't ignore the doubt lingering behind Erin's question. "It's an event planner position with one of the most reputable firms in this part of the country. Charlotte is so much larger than Meadow Springs. I could plan weddings. Just weddings, with no farm to manage. It's exactly what I've always wanted. They want to buy Magnolia Lane, too, which would be a huge help with my dad's care."

Her justification sounded so empty now.

"Did they make an offer?"

Natalie nodded.

"Oh, man." Erin sighed. "Have you told your parents?"

"Not yet." That conversation would be the hardest.

"Have you accepted?"

"I countered their original offer. They verbally accepted. That's what the phone call was about."

A woman's voice over the intercom summoned a

physician to the radiology department, interrupting Erin's next question. Then the doors parted again, and Natalie knew by Erin's expression that Shay had arrived.

She swiveled in her seat to find him standing in the middle of the waiting room, hands fisted at his sides. "What are you doing here?"

Natalie pushed to her feet and dared to move closer. "How's Aiden?"

"He's going to be fine, no thanks to you."

His words stung, but she refused to let his anger discourage her. "What a relief. I can't begin to tell you how sorry I am. Kelly had no idea about—"

"You're something else, you know that?" A vein bulged purple in the center of his forehead. "Don't feed me these half-hearted apologies and pretend like it was a minor accident. Which part of life-threatening peanut allergy did you not understand? He could've *died*, Natalie."

"I know. I'm sorry. I should've never answered that phone call."

"A phone call?" Shay's voice grew louder, drawing stares from curious onlookers. "You were on the *phone* while my son helped himself to a lethal snack?"

Natalie cringed. "No, that's not what happened. I mean, yes, I did answer, but I thought I'd quickly accept the job offer, and then I—never mind. I'm so very sorry. What can I do to help?"

"You can leave. Now."

"Shay, please." Her voice fell to a whisper. "I never meant to hurt anyone."

"Too late." His green eyes flashed. "Caroline will get your stuff from my house and drop it by your place. I don't want you anywhere near my family."

He turned away, his long strides carrying him back into the restricted area and out of her life. Natalie sank into the nearest chair, buried her face in her hands and let the tears flow.

Chapter Fifteen

Shay sat beside Aiden's bed in the hospital room, watching the little boy's chest rise and fall while he slept. His own eyelids were growing heavy, but he refused to give in, even though he longed to put this horrible day behind him. He wouldn't close his eyes until the physician came by on evening rounds and reassured him that Aiden's oxygen levels looked good.

The fluorescent lamp mounted on the wall above Aiden's bed cast a harsh light on the portable crib wedged in the corner. Liam shifted, flopping one arm over his head, a contented sigh escaping his lips. Poor kid. He'd been through it today, too. Now he couldn't even sleep in the comfort of his own bed because there wasn't anyone to watch him. Truth be told, plenty of folks had offered to take Liam home, but Shay couldn't let him out of his sight, either.

Getting up from the vinyl recliner, he bypassed

the small table containing a tray from the cafeteria. Aiden and Liam had inhaled the Jell-O and pudding the nurse offered them earlier. He hadn't shared their enthusiasm for what the hospital tried to pass off as beef stew and a garden salad. Bracing one hand against the wall beside the window, he stared out into the darkness. The lighted sign from his favorite fast-food restaurant taunted him from less than a block away. But he wouldn't leave. Not without his boys.

Someone tapped on the door. He turned as it swung open. Mom rushed in, scanning the room. When she saw Aiden, her features crumpled.

"Oh, honey." She crossed to where Shay stood and wrapped her arms around his waist. "We left Boone as soon as you called. How is he?"

Shay patted her back, the slick fabric of her down jacket cold against his fingertips. "He seems to be fine. The doctors want to keep him overnight for observation."

Mom pulled back, her eyes glistening in the semidarkness as she looked at him. "How are you holding up?"

He shrugged, words failing him as Dad lowered a paper grocery bag to the floor and then approached Aiden's bedside. His Adam's apple bobbed up and down as he stared at his grandson, fingers wrapped tightly around the metal railing. This was the most emotion, other than frustration, Dad had expressed in weeks.

"I'm okay." Shay jammed his hands in his pockets. "I hate that they have to stay here tonight."

She tiptoed over to the crib and peeked down at Liam. "Why don't you go home and get some rest? Your father and I can stay here."

"No."

Dad cleared his throat. "It's no trouble. You'll feel better if you eat a decent meal and get some rest. Hospitals are lousy for sleeping."

His parents certainly knew a thing or two about hospital life. They'd taken turns staying with his little brother around the clock. A revolving cast of distant relatives had come and gone from the house, speaking in hushed voices and offering him his favorite foods. Didn't they understand? All he'd wanted was for life to go back to normal. But everything changed that summer.

Shay returned to his post in the miserable recliner. "I can't leave. Not without them."

Mom stood next to Dad, tucking her arm in the crook of his elbow. "We understand how you feel."

Dad pinched his lips into a thin line, shaking his head. "Watching your child lie here is the most helpless feeling in the world. You'd give anything to trade places."

His words stabbed at Shay. The old familiar feelings of guilt and remorse reared their ugly heads. A sour taste climbed up the back of his throat. "I'm sorry I couldn't save him."

Mom's mouth dropped open. Her eyes flitted

from Dad to him. "Is that what you think? That we blame you for your brother's death?"

"I'm the one who convinced Eric to swim out that far." He'd teased him mercilessly, calling him a baby and a sissy, until his brother dove into the water, arms flailing as he swam toward the float anchored in the middle of the pond.

"But I'm the parent, and I was supposed to be watching both of you, not talking to my friends."

"I tried so hard to tow him back to shore." Shay squeezed his eyes shut. "He wasn't talking anymore, even though I kept telling him he couldn't give up."

Mom and Dad's footsteps shuffled on the floor as they rounded Aiden's bed and stood on either side of Shay, the warmth of their hands on his shoulders bringing him the comfort he craved.

"Son, we never blamed you." Dad's voice was gruff. "I'm sorry you've carried that burden all this time."

Swiping at the moisture dripping from his nose, Shay raised his head. "If you didn't blame me, then why did you send me away?"

Mom's sharp intake of breath revealed her shock. "We didn't think you'd be able to handle living overseas on the heels of losing your only sibling."

"Boarding school separated you from us, but it also offered stability and a phenomenal education." The crevices on Dad's forehead deepened. "It was one of the toughest decisions we've ever made. But when we came home from overseas and saw what a fine young man you were becoming, we thought we'd made the right choice."

Shay turned this information over in his mind. So it wasn't a punishment, after all. In the midst of their own heartache, they'd made a difficult decision to leave him in someone else's care so he'd have the best chance at success. Although the feelings of abandonment he'd struggled with for so long still lingered, staring at his own precious children, he began to see his parents' motivations in a new light.

Pushing to his feet, he embraced Mom first and then stepped closer to Dad. They'd never been much for hugging. "I don't completely understand your decisions, but I respect you for doing what you thought was best."

Dad looked away, struggling to maintain his composure. He reached over and patted Shay's shoulder awkwardly. "It's a shame it's taken more than twenty years for us to have this conversation. That's my fault. I'm afraid I've let my struggles with my own grief get in the way of my relationship with you. I'm sorry. Please forgive me. Eric's death was a tragedy, not your responsibility."

Shay swallowed hard, nodding. It wasn't much. But it was a start. He'd take it.

Mom rubbed her hand across Shay's back. "We love you and your boys. I'm sorry you've suffered in silence."

"I love you, too." Shay leaned down and dropped a kiss on her hair. "I could've said something a long time ago."

She swiped at her tears with her fingertips. "Sometimes hard circumstances lead to the most important conversations."

Unable to speak past the lump clogging his throat, Shay lowered himself to the chair.

"You must be exhausted." Mom adjusted the sheet covering Aiden's legs. "Why don't you let us stay here while you go home and rest?"

"I can't sleep knowing my children are here."

"We could take Liam with us," Dad said. "Then you'd be able to focus all of your attention on Aiden."

"It's no trouble," Mom said. "We have the extra car seat you gave us."

Shay reached for his keys and then hesitated. "I can't. Thank you for offering. Why don't you go home? I promise I'll call if anything changes."

Aiden's eyes fluttered open, and he glanced around the room, a mixture of surprise and panic flooding his little face.

"Hey, buddy," Shay whispered, jumping to his feet. "It's okay. You're safe now."

His little lip pooched out, and a tear trickled from the corner of his eye. Shay's heart ached as he cupped Aiden's hand in his own. Across the room, Liam woke up and began to cry, too.

"Oh, dear." Mom turned and scooped Liam into

her arms. "It's scary in here, isn't it? Let Nana hold you for a few minutes, okay? You and your brother are going to be just fine."

"Nat-lee?" Aiden craned his neck. "Nat-lee?"

Mom's brow knitted together as she carried Liam over to the side of Aiden's bed. "What's he saying?"

"Nat-lee. Want Nat-lee," Aiden cried, louder this time.

Shay's chest tightened. "He's asking for Natalie, the woman who was supposed to be taking care of them."

Their interaction in the waiting room earlier flashed in his mind. As her words echoed back, a fresh wave of anger crested. *A job offer?* He gritted his teeth. When did she plan to tell him about that? She'd said "accepted," which meant she'd probably known about it for quite a while. The realization knifed at his heart. How could he be so stupid to fall for another woman who only put her aspirations first?

"Is she here?"

"No." Shay grabbed one of the new stuffed animals the nurse had brought earlier and handed it to Aiden. "She's not here, buddy. How about your new tiger? Want to hold him?"

"No, no, no." Aiden knocked the stuffed tiger out of Shay's hand. "Nat-leeee."

Determined not to lose his temper, Shay pulled Aiden into his arms and tried to soothe him.

"Is there anything we can do?" Mom settled Liam against her shoulder and swayed back and forth.

"Want me to go find Natalie?" Dad pulled his keys from his pocket.

"Absolutely not." Shay fought to keep his tone even as he smoothed Aiden's hair with his hand. That was out of the question. If she hadn't been so careless, they wouldn't be in this situation. He meant what he'd said in the waiting room. From now on, he wanted nothing to do with her. Despite all the warnings, he'd taken a risk and opened his heart. Look where it got him. He'd nearly lost Aiden. The sooner the boys forgot about Natalie, the better.

Muffled voices summoned Natalie from a deep sleep. Bright light burst through the curtains, and she burrowed farther under her quilt to block out both intruders. *How could it possibly be morning already?*

Someone knocked on her bedroom door. "Natalie?"

Kirsten. Here. Now. If she saw the boxes and packing material scattered around the kitchen—

"Natalie? Are you all right? We need to talk."

Natalie sat up and scrubbed her palm across her face. Then she glanced at the alarm clock on her nightstand. Ten fifteen. She'd totally overslept. No wonder her sisters had come looking for her. They'd agreed to meet at nine this morning, and she'd planned to break the news about Forever Love's offer.

"Nat?" Kirsten's voice was more insistent this time.

"Coming." Natalie slipped out of bed, shivering as her bare feet touched the cool hardwood floor. She pulled a hoodie over her pajamas as she crossed to the door and then opened it. "Hey."

"What's going on?" Kirsten crossed her arms over her chest. "What's with the boxes?"

"You're moving, aren't you?" Cami stood behind Kirsten, firing an accusing glare in Natalie's direction. "This is about that job, isn't it?"

"What job?" Tisha moved closer, too, eyes wide.

Natalie sagged against the door frame. The three of them standing there, a mixture of disbelief and accusation on their faces, ushered in another round of doubts. Not to mention more agony over breaking the news to her family. Somehow, in all her daydreaming about the future, she'd never imagined it being this difficult.

"I—I've been offered a job in Charlotte at an event planning firm. They want to buy Magnolia Lane, too. One of the owners called while I was babysitting the boys. Then the peanut thing happened, and I just didn't get a chance to tell—"

"What peanut thing?"

"You were babysitting?"

"Wait. You're selling Magnolia Lane?"

The questions came rapid-fire.

"Here." Tisha angled her head toward the living room. "Why don't we all sit down? I'll make some coffee, and you can give us the details."

Natalie nodded. "Caffeine would be good. Thank you."

"What about Mama and Daddy?" Cami sank into the chair in the corner. "Should we call them?"

"Please wait." Natalie sat on one end of the sofa while Kirsten took the opposite end. "I—I know I need to speak with them. I just need a few minutes to gather my thoughts."

"They're going to be shocked." Kirsten frowned, hugging a throw pillow to her chest.

"I know." Natalie groaned and tipped her head back, staring at the ceiling. "I already signed the counteroffer and sent it back. It's a lot of money, y'all. An offer that's too good to pass up."

"How much?" Kirsten asked.

Natalie met her sisters' curious gazes. "Two hundred and fifty thousand dollars."

"You're kidding." Cami's eyes widened. "That's insane."

At least one person didn't think she was nuts.

"But that includes the barn and the two acres, right?" Kirsten sighed and shook her head. "Mama and Daddy aren't going to be happy about that."

"Please don't say that to me," Natalie pleaded. She'd convinced herself this was the right thing to do. Why couldn't they be supportive?

The single-serve coffee maker in the kitchen

pumped and whirred. Tisha came into the living room a moment later with a steaming mug. She offered it to Natalie. "Here you go. Would anyone else like some?"

"No, thanks." Kirsten waved her off.

"I'll get some in a minute." Cami fidgeted with the zipper on her hoodie. "I want to hear more about Natalie's move."

Tisha sat on the floor and gently scooted an empty cardboard box out of the way. "Please tell us more about this offer."

Natalie set her coffee on a coaster and mustered the courage to explain. "Since I've opened Magnolia Lane, my favorite part of the business has been the weddings and receptions. I love being a part of those celebrations. But managing the farm and doing the event planning on the side has pulled me in two different directions. Enough is enough. I can't do it anymore. This is my chance to finally live out my dream and focus exclusively on wedding planning."

"What if I volunteered to take your place managing the farm?" Cami hugged her knees to her chest. "Would you stay?"

"No." Natalie shook her head. "It's time for a fresh start. This is a wonderful opportunity, and I'd be crazy to turn it down."

"The guy with the cute little boys?" Kirsten prodded. "What does he think of all this?"

Natalie shrugged and stared at the floor. "It doesn't matter. He never wants to see me again."

"No way." Kirsten leaned over and squeezed Natalie's shoulder. "What happened?"

"Is this about the babysitting and the peanut thing?" Tisha asked.

Natalie squeezed her eyes shut. "Yes."

"I saw Caroline, and she asked how you were handling things," Tisha said. "When I didn't know what she meant, she kind of filled me in."

Natalie opened her eyes. "Shay didn't have anyone to watch the boys over the weekend, and trading shifts or calling in sick wasn't an option, so I was his last resort for a babysitter. Long story short, I got distracted by a phone call, and someone gave one of the boys something with peanuts in it, and he had a severe reaction. Ambulance ride to the ER, admitted for observation..."

Kirsten groaned. "I'm so sorry. That must've been terrifying."

"It was horrible." A shiver raked Natalie's spine as she recalled those tense moments. "Needless to say, Shay is livid. Told me Aiden could've died and he never wants to see me again."

"I'm sure he doesn't mean that," Tisha said. "We say some pretty awful things when we're angry."

"He's right, though. Aiden could've died. I shouldn't have been so easily distracted." Natalie bit her lower lip. If only she could do it over again. She never would've answered the phone.

"Not to make you feel worse, but are you sure this is the best time to move away?" Kirsten asked. "With Daddy's health the way it is, I'm concerned—"

"You heard Mama. She said she'll handle Daddy's care." Natalie took a sip of her coffee. "I won't be so far away that I can't come home if necessary. Like I said, the money from the acquisition will help pay for Daddy's long-term needs."

At least, that's what she kept telling herself.

"As someone who has left and then come back, I can tell you there's definitely an upside to experiencing life outside of Meadow Springs." Tisha offered a kind smile. "I know you and I haven't always agreed on the way things should be done. Please know that I support your decision to go and chase your dream."

Natalie couldn't hide her surprise. "Thank you, Tisha. That's the nicest thing you've said to me in a long time."

"You're welcome."

"It sounds like you've made up your mind." Kirsten released a heavy sigh. "What will happen to Magnolia Lane once the sale is final?"

"Forever Love wants to absorb it into their business. I won't—"

"So that's it?" Cami's gaze flitted around the room. "I'm going to help manage the farm, and you're going to move to Charlotte? Somebody else will be in charge of your precious venue?"

"When the deal is finalized, Forever Love will own the barn. I'll still have quite a bit of input, though." At least, she hoped she would. Even if another associate coordinated the weddings, they'd still need Natalie's insights, wouldn't they?

"When are you going to tell Mama and Daddy?" Cami asked.

"Today." Natalie twisted the hem of her pajama top around her finger. She couldn't put it off any longer.

"Mama will try to talk you out of it," Tisha said.

"It won't work. I have to go." She lifted her chin, determined. Shay had made his feelings very clear. She had no reason to stay. Charlotte provided an escape—a place to start over where she wouldn't see Shay and his boys anymore. Maybe someday, months from now, she'd be able to forget how much they meant to her.

Chapter Sixteen

Shay tugged the wet clothes out of the washer and shoved them into the dryer, the familiar scent of detergent filling his nostrils. How could two little people generate so many loads of laundry? He closed the door and punched the buttons to start the machine. What a way to spend a Friday night. Alone and doing chores.

You didn't have to be alone tonight. Caroline invited you to a party.

"Yeah, right," he muttered as he strode into the kitchen. Natalie's going-away party sounded anything but festive. He wasn't in the mood to celebrate her unexpected departure. The anger over the news that she'd accepted a job in Charlotte had subsided. If he was honest, her choice had completely wrecked him, confirmed what he'd suspected—he shouldn't have spewed those ugly words at her in the waiting room. Shame washed over him. He'd do anything to take it all back. Make things right. Convince her to change her mind.

He raked his hand through his hair and then leaned against the counter, the unwanted yet familiar ache of regret seeping into his heart. The boys had been asleep for a couple of hours already. But the peace he once longed for at the end of the day did little to soothe him. Instead, it magnified his loneliness. While declining Caroline's invitation seemed like a good idea at the time, he felt foolish now. In the days following the incident at the park, he'd felt justified clinging to his convictions. After all, Natalie's careless actions had almost caused the unthinkable. But those thoughts only made him weary, and the hole left by her absence in his life had expanded to a cavernous void.

He pushed off from the counter and wandered into the family room. The twinkling lights on the Christmas tree in the corner filled the room with a soft glow, normally one of his favorite parts of the season. But tonight, all he saw were the blank spaces on the limbs where the boys had plucked ornaments and then hid them. He probably should've thought of that before he hung the shiny temptations within reach of toddlers. As he dropped to his hands and knees and crawled around to retrieve ornaments from under the tree, inside the wicker magazine basket and the side-table drawer, his thoughts circled back to Natalie.

She didn't intentionally set out to harm Aiden or

Liam. Until the boys were older—much older—and could advocate for themselves by refusing snacks containing potential allergens, they needed adults to intervene and protect them. Natalie had helped him care for the boys when he didn't have anyone else to ask. Based on the way he'd seen her interact with others, and the concerns she expressed for her own family, she'd probably been very attentive to their needs and only stepped away for an instant. She couldn't possibly have known a stranger would give the boys food without asking permission first. It could've happened to the most vigilant of caregivers. Even him.

Too bad she was leaving town in less than twenty-four hours and he was on shift tomorrow. He longed to tell her everything that was on his mind. He shouldn't have been so judgmental. Sure, he hated that she'd considered a job offer without telling him. Falling in love with a woman who had chosen her career over him felt painfully familiar.

But maybe the pain had a purpose. He'd let his pride get in the way far too many times and hadn't fought hard enough to save his relationship with Monica. That was a mistake he wasn't about to make twice. He'd spent the last several months trying his best to go it alone.

And hating every minute of it.

Lord, please help me make sense of this. I know there's a place in my world and my heart for Natalie.

He'd been the selfish one, so focused on his own

fears that he couldn't see the beautiful gift of a second chance at love that the Lord had practically dropped in his path.

Shay returned the last of the ornaments to the tree, hanging them all just a little higher this time. Then he stood to survey his work. His gaze landed on a new ornament, a picture frame with the current year stamped on the bottom edge. A picture of him and the boys together at the farm filled the tiny square. Emotion clogged his throat. Mom must've done this for him. How he wished Natalie was in the photo, too.

He owed her an apology for the harsh words he'd spoken and his stubborn determination to shut her out. If only he could convince her to change her mind—not just about dating a firefighter again but staying in Meadow Springs, too. Taking a leap of faith. Together. He understood her desire to follow her dreams, and he certainly wouldn't stand in her way. Did she need to move to have what she longed for, though? Could operating Magnolia Lane *and* building a life with him and his boys ever be enough?

But you haven't given her a reason to stay.

The realization felt like a punch in his gut. He'd wasted so much precious time. He hoped and prayed it wasn't too late for a second chance.

"Are you sure this is what you want?" Mama dabbed at her eyes with a tissue.

Natalie smiled through her own tears and gestured to the loaded U-Haul trailer hitched to her SUV. "It's a little late to change my mind, don't you think?"

"Never." Daddy's eyes glistened, too. The tip of his cane bumped against the asphalt as he moved closer, his other hand sliding along the side of the trailer for extra support. "We want you to follow your heart. If this isn't what you want, speak up." He paused, lips trembling as he searched for the words. "I'll send your sisters to move you back."

"No. I'm going." The lump in her throat grew larger. She had to get out of here before Daddy's tender words derailed her best efforts to keep her fragile emotions in check. She'd made her decision. Charlotte meant a fresh start and her dream job— everything she said she wanted. Right?

Erin stepped forward, a white cardboard box in one hand and an insulated travel mug in the other. "Sustenance for the drive."

"You didn't have to do that." Natalie lifted the lid and peeked inside. An assortment of cookies and her favorite banana chocolate chip muffins were nestled on a bed of wax paper. The sugary scent of the treats mingled with the faint aroma of coffee wafting from the mug. Her stomach growled in response.

"Here." Erin took the treats back. "Hug your sisters while I stash these where you can reach them."

Tisha, Cami and Kirsten huddled in a semicircle,

their eyes red-rimmed. Natalie felt like her heart might split in two. "Y'all, don't look so sad. This isn't goodbye forever. I'll be back for Christmas, remember?"

Kirsten pulled her into a fierce hug. "I'm happy for you. But it's so hard to see you go. Post lots of pictures online. I want to see your new place."

"I will." She moved on to Cami. "I'm proud of you, little sister. Thanks for spending your winter break working here."

"You're welcome." Cami's lip trembled. "I'll probably call you for lots of advice."

"Whatever. You don't need any tips from me. You're going to rock it." Natalie gave Cami's arm one last pat and then faced Tisha.

"Thank you for staying on and managing the farm." She offered Tisha a hug.

"I'm happy to be here." Tisha gave her a tender squeeze. "Have a safe trip."

Natalie pulled back, meeting Tisha's gaze. "I'm sorry I was so hard on you. Daddy's right. You are the perfect person to keep things running smoothly around here."

"You had every right to be concerned." She dragged her fingertips beneath her eyes. "All is forgiven. The past is exactly where it should be—in the past."

Natalie nodded and glanced at Rex, Nolan, Shelby and Bridget lined up beside Erin, looking absolutely pitiful. She couldn't take much more of this. After quickly saying goodbye to them, she stopped in front of her best friend.

The tears couldn't be staunched any longer. Erin folded her into a warm hug. "I'm going to miss you, friend. Take care of yourself."

"Miss you, too," she whispered. Natalie moved quickly to her SUV, eager to get on the road and put all this sadness behind her. Literally. Wasn't there supposed to be some joy and anticipation involved in starting a new adventure?

Mama and Daddy stood next to her open door, clinging to each other. Tears dampened their cheeks. Many difficult conversations had occurred in recent days. They'd given her their blessing to go, but confusion still lingered in their eyes. "I love you, Mama. See you soon."

"I love you, too, sugar. Let us know when you get there." Mama patted her hand.

"Proud of you." Daddy let go of his cane and enveloped her in a tight hug, his body trembling.

Natalie wept. Daddy's health topped her short list of reasons to question her decision.

"Bye, Daddy." She pressed a kiss to his cheek and then turned to leave. With one foot on the running board, and her hand on the door frame, she took one last look around. It wasn't just about appreciating the view of the farm and the faces of the people she loved. Her hesitation was more about what she didn't see. No little blond boys and their handsome firefighter dad had come to see her off.

Shay hadn't made an appearance at her going-away party the night before, either.

He could've died, Natalie.

She winced. His words from the emergency room still echoed in her thoughts. Her careless actions had obviously ruined any hope of a relationship with him. So why stay?

She banished the lonely ache that accompanied thoughts of him and slid behind the wheel. She pulled the door closed, started the engine and waved goodbye to her family and friends as she drove away.

At the farm's exit, she smiled through her tears at the trio of giant Christmas trees her sisters had fashioned for the holiday season. They looked amazing next to the new sign Kirsten added, welcoming visitors to the farm to enjoy the Christmas lights extravaganza. Two nights ago, they'd had record-breaking crowds. Clearly the farm would be fine without her.

Mopping at her tears with one of the napkins Erin provided, she took a sip of her coffee and then eased onto the highway. *Am I going to be okay without the farm?*

That was a question she hadn't considered until everything she loved and cared about filled her rearview mirror.

Well, not exactly everything.

No matter how many times she vowed not to

think about him, Shay worked his way back into her mind.

"Enough," she whispered and turned on the radio, her favorite country station blasting from the speakers.

Cruising down Main Street, she caught sight of a fire engine parked at the gas station. She stared straight ahead, refusing to check if a certain blond-haired man in uniform was in the cab. Pressing her foot down on the accelerator, she drove toward the interstate. This time, she didn't look back.

Shay squeezed the handle on the gas pump to start the flow of diesel into the fire engine's tank. Nothing happened. He stared at the digital screen on the pump. *Invalid PIN code.*

C'mon, concentrate.

Frowning, he inserted the debit card into the machine again and then reentered the PIN number Chief Murphy told him to use. Since he'd decided to try to speak to Natalie one more time, he'd been so distracted. Anxious, too. Somehow, he needed to come up with a plausible excuse to stop by the farm before she left. *Please, Lord, help me figure something out. Quickly.*

Trent came out of the convenience store, carrying two bottles of soda, his brow furrowed. "You okay, man?"

"Yeah." Shay put the card back in his wallet. "Tired, I guess."

"We missed you at the party last night."

"I wasn't in the mood."

"No kidding." Trent studied him. "If it's any consolation, I don't think Natalie's all that excited about leaving, either."

Shay pivoted and stared at the numbers on the pump clicking upward. "I…" A response died on his lips as Trent's words sank in, fanning the embers of hope still flickering in his heart. Was this the second chance he'd hoped for?

"You aren't going to say goodbye before she leaves?"

"I wanted to, but—"

"What if you had another opportunity?"

Shay met Trent's piercing gaze again. "Such as?"

Trent angled his head toward the road. "She just drove by."

Shay whipped around, scanning Main Street. The tail end of a U-Haul trailer behind a familiar SUV was barely visible in the distance. *Too late. Again.*

The pump clicked off, indicating the tank was full. He hated the sickening feeling lodged in the pit of his stomach. Natalie's beautiful smile and mesmerizing eyes flashed in his memory, and he knew he wasn't over her. Not by a long shot.

"If we hurry, we can still catch her."

"What are you talking about?"

Trent took the pump from him and put it away. "Official fire department business. I'll drive."

"We're going to pull her over?"

Trent grinned. "Have you got a better idea?"

They jumped in the cab, and Trent turned on the ignition.

Shay buckled his seat belt. "This isn't going to go over well with the chief."

"Are you sure about that?" Trent turned on the siren and then pulled onto Main Street. "We're worried about you, man. Murphy most of all."

"Then you'd better find a way around this." Shay's pulse ramped up as he gestured toward the line of cars inching along from the intersection of Main and First, in town, all the way to the on-ramp for the freeway. *Stupid morning commute.*

"No worries." Trent leaned on the horn as he expertly maneuvered around the backup. "We've got this equipment at our disposal—might as well use it."

Shay could only grunt in response. By the time they merged onto the freeway, his heart was about to pound right out of his chest. This was crazy. If they caught up, why would Natalie even pull over?

"There." Trent pointed through the windshield. Natalie drove in the far-right lane, about six car lengths ahead. "Are you ready?"

"As ready as I'll ever be."

Trent sped up until he was uncomfortably close to the bumper of her trailer, the fire engine's siren continuing its obnoxious wail.

"C'mon, pull over," Shay murmured.

Finally Natalie's blinker clicked on, and she slowly eased past the white line and onto the shoulder.

Trent slowed to a stop and cut off the siren, but let the lights keep flashing. "You've got this."

Shay whispered a prayer for the right words and Natalie's willingness to listen. Then he jumped out of the cab and jogged toward her side of the SUV.

Natalie's face registered surprise as she powered down the window. "Shay? What's going on?"

"I'm sorry." He'd said those two words a lot over the past few months. And he'd keep right on saying them if it meant she'd turn that car around.

Those beautiful eyes widened. "For what?"

"I'm sorry I blamed you for Aiden's accident. It could've happened to anyone. Given my own experience with my brother's death, I'm the last person who should be holding something like this against you. Telling you to stay away from my family was cruel and inexcusable. I'm sorry I let my fear and issues about the past come between us."

"Go on."

"You've been nothing but kind, considerate and patient. I regret that I was so blinded by my unreasonable expectations that I didn't appreciate what it meant to have you in my life."

"Apology accepted." She tightened her grip on the steering wheel and checked her mirrors. "Un-

less my trailer's on fire or something, I'm afraid I
need to get—"

"Stay."

She sucked in a breath. "W-what did you say?"

"Please don't go. Give us—me and my boys—
another chance."

Cars flew by, the hum of their tires on the asphalt filling the uncertain silence between them.
A stiff breeze trailed in their wake, rippling the
pant legs of his uniform as he waited in agony for
her response.

"You're asking a lot."

"You're giving up a lot. Family, friends, the future of Magnolia Lane. Can whatever's in Charlotte
compete with all of that?"

Her lower lip trembled. "I—I accepted the offer
because I didn't think you wanted me."

No.

Shay swallowed hard. "You have every right to
tell me to get lost after what I said to you. If this
job is all you've ever dreamed about, and you can't
say no, I don't want to stand in your way. But if
there's a possibility that your dreams might come
true right here in Meadow Springs, please turn this
thing around." He reached through the open window and covered her hand with his. "I love you,
Natalie."

A sheen of moisture turned her eyes a captivat-
ing shade of blue. "I love you, too."

Shay's heart hammered. He scanned her face, afraid he'd misunderstood. "What does this mean for us?"

"It means I'd be miserable without you if I left now."

"But didn't you already accept an offer?"

"The contract says I have until today to change my mind."

"You'll still be able to keep Magnolia Lane?"

She nodded. "If I call them today and back out."

A wave of relief washed over him. He reached up and tucked a wayward strand of hair behind her ear and then caressed her cheek with his thumb. "Could I ask you to step out of your car?"

"I thought you were a fireman. You sound like a cop."

"This will just take a second."

Natalie pushed the door open and slid to the ground. "Thank you for coming after me. It isn't every day a girl gets chased down by a handsome man in uniform."

"I'd chase you all the way to Charlotte if I had to."

Those perfect pink lips of hers formed a hopeful smile. "You would?"

"Absolutely." He pulled her into his arms, savoring the familiar scent of her perfume and the way she fit perfectly against him. "Have I mentioned how much I adore you?"

She roped her arms around his neck, and her gaze shifted to his lips. "Tell me again."

He lowered his head, claiming her mouth with his, and showed her he had no intention of letting her go.

Epilogue

One Year Later

Christmas music streamed from the portable speaker on the kitchen table in Natalie's bungalow. She tugged a piece of tape from the dispenser and secured the wrapping paper on the cardboard box. Humming along to "Little Drummer Boy," she added a shiny red bow and then scrawled Aiden's name on the gift tag. Perfect. She stacked it next to an identical gift for Liam. Brand-new dump trucks would be perfect for the sandbox Warren and Belinda were giving the boys for Christmas.

The muffled sound of footsteps on her porch made her smile. Good thing she'd finished wrapping those gifts. She slipped her arms through her heavy peacoat and then wrapped a plaid scarf around her neck. After a busy week coordinating last-minute details for all three of the December brides hosting receptions at Magnolia Lane, a night out at the farm enjoying the Christmas lights with Shay and the boys was exactly what she needed. Later, they'd stop by Erin and Derek's Christmas party—another one of Natalie's favorite Meadow Springs traditions.

The doorbell chimed, setting butterflies loose in her abdomen. Between her packed schedule and his shift at the fire station, it had been two long days since she'd seen Shay. Held his hand. Savored the sweet words he whispered in her ear.

She crossed the hall in three quick strides, untucking her hair from her scarf as she walked. Twisting the handle, she pulled open the door. A blast of cold air greeted her.

Shay stood on the porch with Aiden and Liam at his side.

"Natalie!" the boys shouted, looking adorable in red down jackets and matching navy blue knit hats.

"Hey, boys. What's going on? Are you ready to look at the lights?"

"Lots of lights." Aiden hopped from one foot to the other. "And it's snowing!"

"Pretty lights." Liam grinned up at her. "Daddy says treats, too. If we're good."

"Treats are my favorite. I'll try to be good." Natalie winked at Shay.

"Hey." He offered that traffic-stopping smile, making her knees go weak. A light dusting of snowflakes clung to the shoulders of his black overcoat.

"I can't believe it's still snowing." She scanned the field behind them. A thick blanket of snow coated the grass between her bungalow and the pond. In the distance, the lights from the Christmas extravaganza twinkled. Visitors to the farm tonight would have a memorable experience. Hopefully they'd ordered plenty of hot cocoa and extra marshmallows.

Oh, wait. That wasn't her problem anymore. Since she'd passed the baton first to Tisha last winter and then officially to Evan—their new manager—after Tisha married Chase, the farm and its many intricacies were no longer her responsibility. She was free to focus exclusively on coordinating weddings at Magnolia Lane. Her rustic barn's unprecedented success had far exceeded anything she'd dreamed of. The Lord had blessed her abundantly, and in the past year, He'd shown her again and again the tremendous freedom of trusting Him with her future. Gone was the heavy burden of self-sufficiency.

She glanced at Shay. "Let me grab my hat."

"My hat. Aiden's hat." Liam patted his head and then pointed to his brother.

"I love your hats." Natalie joined them on the porch as she tugged her hat into place. "Did you play in the snow today?"

"No." Shay pulled her door shut. "At this rate, there will be plenty to play in tomorrow."

"True. Maybe you can build snowmen." She stepped off the porch and tipped her head back. Thick flakes fell from the sky. She couldn't resist sticking out her tongue and catching a few. The boys giggled and tried to imitate her.

"I hate to break up the fun, but I think I hear something coming," Shay said.

Natalie turned and surveyed the semidarkness beyond the glow of her porch light. "You do?"

"Listen." He pressed his finger to his lips.

She tilted her head. The unmistakable sound of sleigh bells jingling moved closer. *What in the world?*

Moments later, two chestnut horses pulling an old-fashioned sleigh stopped in front of the porch. Rex sat on the bench seat, holding the reins. "Evening, folks."

Natalie cupped her hand over her mouth and stared up at Shay.

He grinned. "Would you like to go for a ride?"

She nodded quickly, too shocked to say anything else. Where did he find a *sleigh*?

"C'mon, hurry." Liam trotted toward the sleigh.

"Wait for me." Aiden ran after him.

"Ladies first." Shay took Natalie's hand in his and helped her up into the sleigh. The boys followed, piling in beside her.

"One second." Shay joined them, unfolding two thick blankets, which he then spread across their laps. She settled next to him and scooted closer, seeking the added warmth of his arm around her shoulders.

"There." Shay pulled the blanket a little tighter. "Whenever you're ready, Rex."

Rex clicked his tongue, and they were off, gliding across the field. Snowflakes clung to her eyelashes, and the chilly air nipped at her cheeks, but she didn't care.

Shay nuzzled her cheek. "Are you cold?"

His breath on her skin sent shivers of delight rippling through her. "Not at all."

As the sleigh picked up speed, Aiden and Liam giggled. Even though Natalie had looked at the lights displayed on the farm dozens of times, it was infinitely more enjoyable with Shay and the boys. Experiencing the view from Aiden and Liam's perspective made her ten times more grateful they were all together.

Rex steered them toward another illuminated design, a complex display of lights that spelled out the words *Merry Christmas*. Aiden and Liam squirmed with delight. Seeing the joy on their faces as the animated displays twinkled and flashed to the beat of the coordinated music made Natalie wish they had twenty more acres of lights to see. She snuggled closer to Shay. "I love seeing them so happy."

"You're partly responsible for that happiness. You know that, right?"

Warmth flooded through her. "It's a privilege to be a part of their lives."

"We'd be lost without you." Shay pressed a quick kiss to her cheek.

The ride ended much too soon. Rex eased to a stop in front of Magnolia Lane. The horses snorted and stomped, tossing their heads and making the bells jingle again.

"Thank you, Rex," Natalie said, pushing the blankets aside.

"Now just a minute, Miss Natalie." Rex stood and climbed down from his seat. Turning, he reached up for Liam and Aiden. "Somebody told me there are cookies and hot cocoa inside for little boys. Wanna go see?"

Liam shot Natalie a questioning glance.

"Must be those treats you were hoping for, buddy. Go check it out." She waited while Rex scooped the boys from the sleigh and then led them toward the livery's entrance.

Shay stretched out his hand and helped her from the sleigh. The snow hadn't eased up at all. She tucked her fingers in the crook of his elbow, and they jogged after Rex and the boys. Natalie burrowed her chin inside her scarf as the flakes sprinkled her nose and cheeks.

Inside the barn, her steps faltered. "Oh, my."

The corridor between the old stalls glowed with hundreds of white twinkle lights. A carpet of rose petals stretched from the toes of her boots to the double doors leading into the reception hall.

"How did you...? When did the...?" She turned around, the questions dying on her lips.

Shay had dropped to one knee, a velvet jewelry box offered up on his open palm.

"Natalie Campbell, I love you with all of my heart. Will you marry me?"

"Yes. A thousand times, yes." A wave of emotions crested inside her. This moment was everything she'd imagined it would be.

Shay stood and slid the platinum diamond ring on her left hand. Only inches separated them. He sealed the proposal with a searching kiss, making her legs tremble.

She sighed as he pulled back. "Thank you. This is amazing. I can't wait to spend the rest of my life with you."

He brought her hand to his lips and brushed her knuckles with another kiss. "I have one more surprise for you."

"What could possibly top this?"

The doors at the opposite end of the corridor slid open, revealing a room packed with all the people she loved the most. Cheers erupted as Shay guided her inside. Liam and Aiden careened across the room, wide smiles lighting up their precious faces. Cookie crumbs and hot cocoa mustaches lined their mouths. Scooping the boys into their arms, they savored the moment together. It was a beautiful start to their happily-ever-after.

* * * * *

*If you enjoyed this story, pick up
these other Love Inspired romances
featuring adorable twins:*

*AMISH CHRISTMAS TWINS
by Patricia Davids
SECRET CHRISTMAS TWINS
by Lee Tobin McClain
TEXAS CHRISTMAS TWINS
by Deb Kastner
THE TEXAN'S TWINS
by Jolene Navarro*

Available now from Love Inspired!

*Find more great reads at
www.LoveInspired.com.*

Dear Reader,

Thank you for reading *The Firefighter's Twins*. It was inspired by a field trip I took with my kids to a former tobacco farm that was transformed into an outdoor playground and pumpkin patch. When we drove past a beautiful restored livery that had become a wedding venue, goose bumps shot down my arms, and suddenly a new plot was germinating. Little did I know all the ways God would challenge me and help me grow as a writer through the creative process. I spontaneously entered this story in Harlequin's Blurb to Book contest, and while I didn't win, the decision to boldly submit my work ultimately led me to becoming a Harlequin Love Inspired author, which is a dream come true.

I think my experience writing this novel is reflected in Natalie's journey as a character. She longs to chase her dreams, yet struggles to trust God's sovereign plan for her life, especially when obstacles arise. I hope Shay and Natalie's story inspires you to step out in faith and chase those big dreams God has planted in your heawrt, as well as cling to the knowledge that God is good and He is always for us.

I love hearing from readers, and you can find me on Facebook, Twitter, Instagram and at HeidiMcCahan.com. All subscribers to my e-newsletter reccive a free novella that isn't available anywhere else. By the way, if you enjoyed *The Firefighter's Twins* and would post an honest review online, I'd be grateful.

Blessings,

Heidi McCahan

HOME on the RANCH

YES! Please send me the **Home on the Ranch Collection** in Larger Print. This collection begins with 3 FREE books and 2 FREE gifts in the first shipment. Along with my 3 free books, I'll also get the next 4 books from the Home on the Ranch Collection, in LARGER PRINT, which I may either return and owe nothing, or keep for the low price of $5.24 U.S./ $5.89 CDN each plus $2.99 for shipping and handling per shipment*. If I decide to continue, about once a month for 8 months I will get 6 or 7 more books, but will only need to pay for 4. That means 2 or 3 books in every shipment will be FREE! If I decide to keep the entire collection, I'll have paid for only 32 books because 19 books are FREE! I understand that accepting the 3 free books and gifts places me under no obligation to buy anything. I can always return a shipment and cancel at any time. My free books and gifts are mine to keep no matter what I decide.

268 HCN 3760 468 HCN 3760

Name	(PLEASE PRINT)	

Address		Apt. #

City	State/Prov.	Zip/Postal Code

Signature (if under 18, a parent or guardian must sign)

Mail to the **Reader Service**:
IN U.S.A.: P.O. Box 1867, Buffalo, NY. 14240-1867
IN CANADA: P.O. Box 609, Fort Erie, Ontario L2A 5X3

* Terms and prices subject to change without notice. Prices do not include applicable taxes. Sales tax applicable in NY. Canadian residents will be charged applicable taxes. This offer is limited to one order per household. All orders subject to approval. Credit or debit balances in a customer's account(s) may be offset by any other outstanding balance owed by or to the customer. Please allow 3 to 4 weeks for delivery. Offer available while quantities last. Offer not available to Quebec residents.